Some Kind of Hell

Frank Zafiro

Other Crime Series By Frank Zafiro

<u>River City Series</u>
Police procedurals with ensemble cast, begins with *Under a Raging Moon*

<u>Sandy Banks Thrillers</u>
Vigilante assassin who targets bad men, begins with *The Last Horseman*

<u>Stefan Kopriva Mysteries</u>
Private detective mysteries, begins with *Waist Deep* (set in River City)

<u>SpoCompton Series</u>
Hardboiled underside of Spokane, begins with *At Their Own Game*

<u>Cam & Bricks Jobs (with Eric Beetner)</u>
Two competing hitmen – action and dark humor, begins with *The Backlist*

<u>Ania Series (with Jim Wilsky)</u>
Hardboiled noir with a femme fatale, begins with *Blood on Blood.*

<u>Charlie-316 series (with Colin Conway)</u>
Police procedurals full of action and intrigue, begins with *Charlie-316*

<u>Jack McCrae Mystery Series</u>
Retired detective solves mysteries, begins with *At This Point in My Life*

<u>A Grifter's Song</u>
Serial anthology series featuring a grifter duo (creator/editor/contributor)

Frank also writes mainstream fiction and non-fiction as Frank Scalise and science-fiction and fantasy as Frank Saverio!

Some Kind of Hell

A Sandy Banks Thriller

Frank Zafiro

Some Kind of Hell: A Sandy Banks Thriller #2

Frank Zafiro

Copyright © 2023 Frank Scalise

Published by Code 4 Press

The characters and events in this book are fictitious. Any similarity to real persons, living or dead, is coincidental and not intended by the author.

Cover Design by Zach McCain

ISBN: 978-1-962889-00-1

For Jack.

Character is destiny.

**— Heraclitus,
Ancient Greek philosopher
544-484 BCE**

1

2011

As they sat on Brophy's patio sipping a beer, Sandy suddenly felt something was wrong. It wasn't that they had fallen silent, nor that their reminiscing abruptly took on a jagged feel to it as they spoke. It was something else. Something external. And dangerous. The realization was like a precipitous temperature drop, invisible yet certain.

Brophy felt it, too. Sandy saw it in his eyes. Both men sensed it, and both had long ago learned the absolute essential lesson of trusting that instinct.

Sandy's mind whirred through possibilities.

Are they deploying?

Already set up?

How long have they been watching?

Are we bugged?

"You get mosquitoes this time of year?" Sandy asked his old friend.

"Not since I moved here." Brophy lifted his nose in the air and sniffed. "But feels like that could change."

"I should probably ex-fil," Sandy said, keeping his tone conversational and his expression unchanged. If they were only being watched and not listened to, he didn't want to tip them off that he knew they were there.

"All right," Brophy agreed easily. He scratched his thick black beard thoughtfully. Then he added, "You probably don't want to take a cab, I figure."

"No," Sandy agreed.

Brophy stood and limped over to the sliding glass door. He slid open the screen and reached around the corner to a key rack near the door. He retrieved a single key on a ring and tossed it to Sandy. "It's for the Jeep in the garage. I'll give you a minute to get behind the wheel."

"What are you going to do?"

"My knock-around-town car is in the driveway," Brophy said. "I think I'll take it to the store. Hell, I might even call back through the front door to my old Army buddy about how I'll be back with more beer soon."

His eyes bore into Sandy's.

"I'll rev twice if I see anything," Brophy added.

Sandy nodded, and followed him inside. As Brophy limped toward the front door, Sandy gathered his few possessions together. He slipped through the kitchen to the door leading to the garage. Once in the garage, he got into the Jeep, quickly rolling down the driver's window. He found the automatic door opener clipped to the visor and rested his thumb on the button, waiting.

Twenty seconds later, he heard Brophy calling to him from the front porch. "Back in ten," came the muffled voice. "7-Eleven is just up the road."

He waited.

A car started on the other side of the garage door. Sandy leaned toward the open window, listening carefully.

The engine revved loudly.

Once.

A moment later, the pitch of the engine changed as Brophy put it in gear. The car pulled away.

One engine rev.

Brophy hadn't seen anything.

That didn't mean there wasn't anything there.

There is. I know it.

Sandy hit the button on the remote. The metal garage door rose in front of him. He started the Jeep, got the feel of the acceleration and tapped the brakes. Once there was enough clearance, he slid the Jeep into gear and shot out of the garage. Without thinking, he pressed the button on the door remote as soon as he was clear.

At the end of Brophy's short driveway, he slowed momentarily. He glanced left. The rear end of Brophy's beater that he used for errands was already two blocks away.

Sandy turned right.

As soon as he pulled onto the street, they emerged. Two cars sprang from the curb up the street to form a V in the roadway. Eight or ten men and women on foot spilled out from various hiding places, including two that burst out from behind Brophy's house. All wore the blue windbreakers favored by the FBI and Marshal's Service and leveled their sidearms at him. One man with a bushy mustache carried a shotgun. He spotted Agent Lori Carter beside him, her gun out and pointed his way. Along with several others, she was shouting orders at Sandy, but their voices were indistinct.

He could see their expressions, though. That told him everything he needed to know. This might have been set up as a capture but it could easily devolve into an execution. Perhaps that was what they preferred, especially Carter.

He'd understand if it was.

That didn't mean he had to accept it.

Sandy gunned the engine and headed straight toward the impromptu barricade.

2

Three days earlier

Special Agent Lori Carter sat on a metal folding chair inside the FBI evidence locker. Boxes filled with paperwork surrounded her. Stray items seized from the residence of Sandy Banks were piled nearby. The open box lay between her feet as she slowly removed each piece of paper and examined it before setting it aside. Once she got through the entire contents of the box, she'd return them, secure the lid, and move on to the next.

This was the third box of the morning.

There were eight more stacked behind her.

Carter sighed. She brushed a stray lock of her dark hair out of her eyes and reached for her coffee. The liquid had gone cold, but she drank it anyway. She glanced at her phone. Her brows went up when she saw it wasn't even technically morning any longer. She'd been at this for hours.

The item in her left hand was a cable bill. She perused it quickly, saw nothing out of the ordinary, and set it aside. Then she dug into the box and withdrew the next piece of evidence.

"Evidence," she muttered dismissively. The crime scene techs had seized any and all paperwork in the entire house, which filled the eleven boxes currently surrounding her. Carter had no one to blame but herself; she'd ordered them to be that thorough. Now, she wasn't exactly *regretting* it, but she was certainly reaping the brunt of the result.

She examined a credit union statement from seven months ago. The figures in Banks's checking and savings accounts ought to be enough to dissuade anyone from going into the hit man business for the money. Not only had her investigation shown the man lived an ascetic, nearly monastic lifestyle, he did so on a shoestring budget. Or he dealt largely in cash. Though, if that was the case, she didn't see signs of him spending any of those elusive funds on anything material.

Maybe he was a true believer, she thought, not for the first time. *A zealot for justice.*

That made her grind her teeth. Vigilante justice was just a rationalization for revenge, as far as she was concerned. While working the Banks case, her partner, Scott, had expressed a looser view. He even went so far as to suggest the people Banks and his crew of ex-cops took out—and *took out* were his words; she said *murdered*—deserved their fates. The world was a better place without them, Scott told her.

She'd detected a whisper of admiration in Scott's words when they had that conversation. Almost as if he halfway approved of what the Four Horsemen were doing for over a decade. At the time, she wrote it off as a ridiculous law enforcement fantasy she suspected a lot of other cops shared as well. But she had a much stricter view of what justice meant. It didn't include being judge, jury, and executioner.

Scott's fascination with Banks melted away when the felon shot him in the thigh after murdering an innocent woman. Those were some of the most terrible moments of Carter's life. Her partner bleeding from an arterial wound while she was in a face-to-face standoff with the serial assassin they were trying to catch.

For whatever reason, Banks had spared her and chosen to flee. She managed to slow Scott's bleeding enough to keep him alive until medics arrived. But she would never forgive Banks for almost killing a good man. His call from the Rutherford Hotel to tip her off to the local cops who were the masterminds of the assassination ring didn't absolve him. Nothing would. That one act of shooting her partner, above all others, had sealed his fate in Carter's mind. She would hunt him mercilessly until he was found and brought to justice.

She'd have to do it without Scott, though. Shortly after he'd awakened and had some time to process the event, her partner told her he was going to put in for a disability retirement. She urged him to give it some time before he decided. But Scott was certain.

"Life is too short to chase shitheads around," he said. "Especially when you have to play by rules and they don't."

"It's the rules that make us better than them," she argued.

"No." Scott shook his head with certainty. "All the rules do is make us lose."

"Scott…"

"None of it matters," he insisted. "I just want to be with my family."

His voice had been so resolute she stopped trying to dissuade him. Instead, she pivoted to being supportive. That was what being a partner meant, at least to her.

While she waited for her feckless boss, Special-Agent-in-Charge (SAC) Edward Maw, to assign her another partner, the closest thing she had to it was her confidential informant (CI), Brian Moore. The former officer and Horseman cut a sweetheart deal, gaining temporary freedom while Banks was at large in exchange for his efforts and cooperation in catching the fugitive.

Carter didn't like Moore. He'd tainted his badge and, by extension, all badges. While she thought his cooperation was beneficial, she knew it was based largely on self-preservation. Only the fact that he'd eventually see time in a federal prison served as some consolation.

She realized she'd been skimming the last few pieces of evidence while lost in her own thoughts. Dutifully, she retrieved them from her done pile and reviewed them again.

A rent receipt from last month.

The warranty for a laptop.

Year-old discharge papers from a minor emergency that showed an ankle sprain.

She paused. The laptop warranty was probably for the one seized from the residence. It was currently with computer forensics, a support unit backed up almost as far as the one processing DNA. She hoped there'd be some clue where Banks might flee on that hard drive. Maybe his Internet search history would prove illuminating.

The door to the evidence room opened and slammed shut. She heard a terse greeting and reply between the clerk and whoever arrived. A moment later, Brian Moore appeared in the doorway to the small storage room. He held up a white bag in his hand.

"Jimmy John's?" he asked.

As if in response, Carter's stomach growled.

Moore grinned and reached into the bag. "I got you Turkey, no mayo," he said.

Carter frowned, but realized she was hungry now, so she accepted the wrapped sandwich when he offered it. Moore dragged another folding chair into the tight confines of the evidence locker and took a seat. Together, they unwrapped their sandwiches and ate in silence.

They were almost finished when Carter asked, "Did you think about what I asked you yesterday?"

Moore finished swallowing a bite before answering. "You mean about family or friends?"

Carter nodded tersely. What else could she have meant? That was the only question she'd asked him to think about over the course of the evening after they finished another meticulous search of Banks's residence.

"No family I ever heard of," Moore said. He took a bite and spoke while he ate. Thankfully, he kept his lips drawn tautly, so she didn't have to see the food while he chewed. "He said once he was an only child. His parents passed away while he was in the military."

"No other relatives?"

"None that were close or that he knew."

That sounded lonely to Carter. She and her sister may not see each other very often, but she still prized the closeness they shared. And she couldn't imagine losing her parents so young.

"Sandy always said that was part of what made him so perfect for Cal's project," Moore said, pushing the last of his sandwich into his mouth and wiping his hands on a napkin.

"That he had no attachments?"

Moore bobbed his head while he chewed. Then he swallowed and added, "Same with me, in a way. I was a late-in-life baby, so my brothers and I were never close. When my parents passed—"

"What about friends?" Carter interrupted.

Moore took the interruption in stride. He paused, thinking. "Outside of the four of us? I don't think he had any. The guy rarely left his house. He was a monk or something."

"You mean hermit," Carter said. "A monk is something

different."

"Either way, he kept pretty much to himself. The rest of us had some kind of life outside of the project, but it didn't seem to me like Sandy did."

Carter frowned. She thought it over while she devoured the remainder of her sandwich. Then she wiped her hands and rolled up the napkin and the wrapper into a tight ball.

Moore held out his hand for the trash. Carter handed it to him and he stuffed it into the white bag with the "JJ" logo on it.

"I did remember one thing," Moore said, setting the bag aside. "I don't know if it'll help, though."

"Try me." Carter reached into the box of paperwork and pulled out the next item.

"Sandy didn't talk about his time in the military hardly at all. He said all he did was guard empty warehouses at Fort Bliss."

Carter grunted, opening the envelope with a ragged edge. Inside she found a bill for car insurance.

"He said it was boring as hell," Moore added.

Carter scanned the insurance bill and dropped it on the done file. She already knew this. While she and Scott were still conducting surveillance, she'd contacted a clerk at the central military records depository. The woman had recounted Banks's unimpressive service record over the phone. *Boring* was a good description.

"He never mentioned any of his army buddies," Moore continued. "Except once. We were drinking pretty heavy one night after Cal died. Sandy raised a glass and toasted Cal for saving his life. Then he said something about the lieutenant being in rare company, along with someone he called Brophy."

"Brophy? You sure?"

Moore nodded. "It stuck in my head for a couple reasons. One, it was kind of a unique name. Two, I knew it wasn't a cop because I knew all the cops on the department. That meant it was probably a soldier. Like I said, he was always tight-lipped about that time of his life."

"Why are you just now telling me this?"

Moore's expression was puzzled. "I just now remembered it."

"You said it stuck in your head."

"Yeah, but not in a big way. It wasn't like meeting Norman Schwarzkopf or something. It was just something he said once that stuck in my brain enough that your question shook it loose."

Carter gave him a dark, appraising look. "If you hold out on me, you know your deal gets rescinded, right?"

Moore blanched. "Jesus, I'm not. I'm trying to help."

"I think you should try harder."

Moore shook his head in amazement. "You're never happy with anything I do."

"That's because you murdered people," she snapped. "And you're getting off easy because you are providing substantial and meaningful information and assistance on this case. Whether your intelligence or efforts are considered substantial and meaningful or not relies heavily on my recommendation. So, do me a favor, and shake loose some more of those memories, huh?"

Moore's face was clouded with dismay. He gave her a short nod. "I understand."

She didn't think he did entirely. For someone who'd been a police officer and a contract killer, Moore seemed to possess a level of naiveté she wouldn't have believed if it hadn't been on display every day since she and Scott scooped up Moore and flipped him into being a confidential informant. She initially thought his lack of guile was contrived. But if the man was acting, his ability to remain in character was impeccable.

Without being told, Moore dug into the evidence box and

began to examine paperwork. Time slowed to a crawl while the pair meticulously sifted through the mundane detritus of the life of Sandy Banks. Carter reached for her cold cup of coffee and sipped the last of the brew.

Moore lifted a small yellow notepad out of the box. He glanced at the empty top page, rifled through the rest to confirm nothing was written and tossed it onto the pile. Carter watched it dispassionately, then turned back to her thick packet of credit card statements.

Then something occurred to her. She picked up the notepad and held it up to the light at an angle. Faint impressions were etched on the paper from whatever Banks had written on now missing sheets. Carter fumbled around in her bag until she found a pencil. She sensed Moore watching her while she gently scribbled back and forth across the surface of the paper.

Letters emerged, white against the dark lead background.

"Holy…" muttered Moore, trailing off in admiration. "Did you learn that at the FBI Academy? Or is that some CIA shit?"

She shook her head. "Some detective show, I think."

When finished, she held the pad at an arm's length and read.

> *Dear Janet,*
> *I know it's been a long time. I'm sorry for that. But I think I'll be home soon. I've missed you, and I love you.*

It was unsigned.

"Who's Janet?" she asked.

"No idea."

Carter turned her gaze upon him. "Remember what I said earlier about full disclosure?"

Moore held up his hands. "As far as I know, Sandy had no women in his life. Maybe he did and he kept it to himself, but it sure as hell never came up in all the time I knew him. I never heard of anyone named Janet."

"You're sure?"

"Positive."

Carter set the notepad aside. She made a few notes on her own steno pad to add Janet to any and all search parameters regarding Banks. The letter sounded like a big deal, so perhaps it would bear fruit.

They returned to the slow process of reviewing documents. Carter waded through the thick stack of credit card statements. She was already back to the late 1990s and was astounded at how similar the statement history was to those from the last few months. The charges each cycle were few and largely predictable. An occasional dinner out. Some small household purchases. Gas and groceries. Nothing noteworthy.

She was about to stand and take a break when she stopped suddenly.

"What is it?" Moore asked her.

Carter felt a small thrill. She knew it might seem like a long shot but, in the midst of so much order and consistency, any aberration screamed importance. She tapped the entry on the credit card statement, in the summer of 1995.

"What?" Moore asked again, impatience creeping into his voice.

"It's a charge from American Airlines," Carter said.

"Sandy flew somewhere?"

"Does that surprise you?"

Moore nodded. "As far as I know, he never left Spokane. When I said he was a monk, I meant it."

"Hermit," Carter corrected absently. She held up the statement. "The charge includes the airport codes."

Moore's face brightened. "What cities?"

"GEG to DEN," she answered. "Spokane to Denver."

Then she looked up at him. "I think there was someone important to him there."

"Family, you think?" He pointed to the notepad near her feet. "Or maybe Janet?"

"Could be," Carter said, but she knew the first thing she was going to do was search the database for anyone in Denver with the last name of Brophy.

3

When Sandy first arrived at Brophy's house, his old friend greeted him warmly.

"Keeg!" he bellowed, reaching out with one meaty paw to clasp Sandy's hand. He drew the smaller man into a clumsy bear hug and clapped him on the back. "I figured I'd never see you again, brother."

"Broph," Sandy said, his voice subdued. Then a warm wash of camaraderie flooded over him. He clutched Brophy back as hard as he could. For a moment, the sensation of belonging, of being understood, completely took over his being.

Brophy let the embrace go on for a few long seconds. His heavy hands thudded on Sandy's back several more times. Then he broke away from the hug but didn't release his grasp on Sandy's hand. If anything, he squeezed harder.

Sandy squeezed back.

"Good to see you," Brophy said thickly. His eyes shone

with unfallen tears.

Sandy cleared his throat. He felt his own eyes burning, as well. "You, too," he said.

Brophy released his hand and slapped him on the shoulder. "Come on. I've got cold beer."

Minutes later, they were on the patio, each sipping a bottle of Coors Light. The years fell away with every word. The two reminisced, sharing laughter and reverence in equal parts. At first, they carefully dodged the land mines that lay in their shared past. Still, Sandy noticed the slight limp in Brophy's gait and he knew, if the old corporal lifted his jeans pant leg, the mottled scar beneath would still be apparent.

No matter how far you run, you take your past with you.

When the conversation steered too close to one of the most painful subjects, Brophy paused. Then he raised his bottle in the air.

"To Evan," he said, his voice husky with emotion.

Sandy raised his own bottle. "To Evan," he agreed.

They drank. Then Brophy chuckled and shook his head.

"What is it?" Sandy asked.

"Nothing. He just deserves to be toasted with something better than this horse piss, that's all."

Sandy shrugged and took another swig. It tasted good to him.

"I've got some Maker's Mark stowed away," Brophy said. "For a special occasion. I'd say this qualifies."

"It's early yet," said Sandy. "Let's pace ourselves."

Brophy chuckled again. "Keegan, it hasn't been *early* for a long time now."

Sandy fell silent. Hearing Brophy utter that name—his Army name—was surreal after all these years. Maybe the old corporal was right. It wasn't early anymore.

"What brings you to Denver?" Brophy asked him. "It's been a minute."

Sandy didn't answer right away. He lifted the bottle and took a pull, thinking about his answer. He'd already put Brophy in danger of being an accomplice by coming here. He knew the man wouldn't care about that. If anything, he'd be upset if Sandy *hadn't* come to him in his hour of need. But how much of the story did his old comrade need to know?

How much did he need to tell?

All of it, Sandy decided. *To both questions.*

But where to start?

"I don't go by Keegan Moore these days," he said.

"I know."

Sandy raised his brow. "You do?"

Brophy nodded. "Saw your plane ticket on the counter when you came to see me that second time… what, twelve years ago? Fifteen?"

"That long?" Sandy said.

"That long," Brophy affirmed. "Time goes fast when you're limping around on a military medical pension. Or playing cops and robbers, for that matter."

"I didn't go straight to that," Sandy told him. "After we discharged, I didn't stay in Texas. I bounced around the country for the better part of a year, trying to figure out what was next."

"Why not go home?"

Sandy winced inside, but he kept an impassive expression. "Not an option."

"All right," Brophy said, seeming to know not to probe. "Why the cops, then?"

Sandy shrugged. "It seemed like I could make a difference doing that. And making a difference was important."

"Did you?"

Sandy thought about it. "Do any of us?"

Brophy laughed. "There's the million dollar question. Here's an easier one, then—why Spokane?"

"That's just where I was when I decided."

Brophy grunted. "I thought they did background checks on cops."

"They do. My DD-214 held up. So did the fake Texas life the Army created for me. It was thin and unremarkable, but it passed muster."

"That makes me feel a little nervous about their hiring process."

"Don't be," Sandy said. "It was the military service that carried the most weight. Think about it—if you're back-grounding a soldier, how far back past his service do you really need to go? You're treading ground the military's already been. They deemed it all good so, at that point, most investigators only give it a cursory look and move on."

"Lucky for you."

"Them, too. I did twelve years in patrol."

"That everything I think it is? You didn't talk about it when you came to visit."

"Most likely." Sandy tipped the bottle and discovered it was empty. Without being asked, Brophy reached into the nearby ice chest and removed another. He gave it to Sandy who popped off the top and raised it toward him. "Nothing as bad as what we saw. For the most part, anyway."

"For the most part," Brophy mused. "Sounds like there's a story somewhere in there."

"Not a good one. I made a mistake. I failed someone."

"We all do, sooner or later," the old corporal said quietly. "I let down Evan."

"*We* let down Evan," Sandy corrected.

Brophy shrugged. "We or me, it all ends the same."

Sandy sipped his beer. "True enough." He let out a long breath. "Afterwards, I thought about quitting. That's when Cal pulled me aside. He told me how I could keep making a difference. There'd be no chance of any mistakes like the one

I made."

"Sounds like he's selling Amway or something."

"He wasn't." Sandy paused, and took another swallow of the beer. "He's gone now, though."

"Oh." Brophy shifted in his seat. "Sorry."

Sandy waved away the apology. "Throat cancer took him a little more than two years into the project."

"Project?"

"The Four Horsemen," Sandy said.

"This Cal guy was a bible reader, huh?"

"I don't know. But we did bring a sort of an apocalypse down on the heads of the people he pointed out."

Brophy peered at him carefully. "So, what are we talking here? Direct action or something?"

"Exactly. Scumbags who slipped the net. He sent us the files and we closed them."

"Jesus, Keegan," Brophy whispered. "You came full circle, brother."

Sandy didn't answer.

"How long?" Brophy asked

"Two years under Cal," Sandy answered. "And another ten under his replacement."

"That's a lot of bodies."

"I didn't look at it that way."

"No? How'd you look at it then?"

"That a lot of victims saw some kind of justice, instead of some kind of hell."

A knowing grin spread across Brophy's face. "Sounds like you found yourself one hell of a rationalization, brother."

"What was the line from that movie? 'Don't knock rationalizations?'"

"Something like that." Brophy drank in silence for a while. Then he asked, "But you're done with that now?"

It was Sandy's turn to grin. "It all went to shit, Broph. I

took out the target, but the brass set me up. It was a civilian. That put the local cops onto me. But the FBI already was. They tried to nab me at the house. I wounded one before I managed to get away. Minus a pit stop to square some accounts with the brass, I've been on the run ever since." His grin returned when he finished, but he injected no humor into it. "So, yes, I'm done."

Brophy nodded, as in approval. He opened his mouth to say something, then stopped.

"What is it?"

After a few moments, he said, "I was gonna say you shouldn't tell me where you're headed after this. Then it occurred to me that I hope it's someplace peaceful. You deserve that."

"We both do," Sandy agreed.

Brophy spread his hands toward his surroundings. "I'm there, brother. At least, as *there* as I'll ever get." He lifted the beer bottle and took a sip. "But I don't get the sense you're headed to some*where*. Feels more like you're headed to some*one*."

Sandy leaned back and tilted his head. "Where'd you get that idea?"

Brophy shrugged. "Just a feeling. But I'm right, aren't I?"

Wordlessly, Sandy nodded.

"You love her?"

"I did," Sandy answered. "Still do, after all these years."

"Sounds like something special."

"It was for me." He cleared his throat. "I knew her before the army."

"Young love, then." Brophy nodded approvingly. "I remember that. Still wrapped up in all that shiny, dreamy shit we all believed when we were kids."

"I think it was more than that." He paused, then added, "I *hope* it was more than that."

"For your sake, I hope it was."

Sandy looked at him. "You say that like you don't believe it."

"I've got no opinion on it. Not specifically. I don't know her and I ain't ever seen you two together. I do know young, lost love seems special to us in our memories because it hasn't ever been tainted by the real world. Never tested, either."

Sandy thought about his words. Then he said, "Maybe you're right. But I know I still feel about her the same way I did when I was eighteen. That's never changed. So, maybe we're just in the middle of that real world test you're talking about. On our way to something else."

"Here's hoping," Brophy said. He clinked the neck of Sandy's bottle with his own and they drank. Then Brophy said, "She's waiting for you, then?"

"I have no idea."

The two of them chuckled at that.

Sandy gave Brophy a slight shrug. "I have to find out, though, right?"

"I suppose you do." Brophy's expression took on a faraway look for a moment. "I envy you," he said. "I had a woman for a few years but it didn't work out. My fault, of course."

"That's what she said?"

"No, that's what I say. I blew it." He took another drink from his bottle. "I don't want to know who or where, brother. But I will say—don't screw it up like I did."

Sandy stared down at his hands. "Hard to screw up what I don't know for sure still exists, Broph. It was a long time ago."

"One thing my mom told me, even years after my dad passed," Brophy said, "is that time doesn't mean much to love." He lifted his hands. "I know, it's cornball as hell, but that doesn't make it untrue. Young love might be an untested illusion, but real love? It stands the test of time."

"You think so?"

"We're sitting here, ain't we?"

"You about to propose to me, Broph?"

"Shit's going to be legal soon enough," Brophy said, smiling. "So, I just might."

Sandy grinned at the joke, but only a little. He took Brophy's point to heart—any true love, romantic or otherwise, tended to outlast the years.

Would it be the same with Janet?

The two men sat quietly. Sandy let all the information soak in for Brophy. He knew the man had other questions, but he would ask and answer many of them in his own head. He waited to see if his friend would ask any more of the kind he couldn't answer for himself.

A full minute passed before Brophy spoke. When he did, his tone was lighter than before. "You like sports?" he asked.

"Sports?" Sandy tilted his head, surprised at the pivot.

"Denver is a sports town," Brophy told him. "We've got whichever one you want here—football, baseball, basketball, hockey… and at least one of the teams is pretty damn good at any given time. Sometimes most of them."

Sandy nodded that he understood. They were done talking about the past. "I always liked baseball the best," he said.

"Really? I've turned into more of a hockey man myself. But you picked the right sport for this time of year. The Rockies are having a decent season so far." Brophy drained his beer and reached for another. "Maybe we'll go catch a game. If you're staying, that is."

"Maybe," Sandy agreed.

They talked baseball for a while. They skipped through the other three sports briefly. Brophy told him about living in Denver. When Sandy asked about his leg, he was matter of fact about the old injury, then changed the subject to the best restaurants in town.

The conversation roamed and the beer flowed.

And then Sandy's instincts suddenly screamed danger. He didn't know why. Maybe he heard something barely perceptible behind the fence. Movement, perhaps. Something that didn't fit. Or a slight variation in the ambient sounds in the neighborhood.

Or maybe that was something his mind filled in when he sensed a change in the air. A vibe, an energy, not unlike the way an animal might catch a scent.

He met Brophy's gaze and held it.

"You get mosquitoes this time of year?" he asked.

4

Sandy drove the Jeep directly toward the two-vehicle barricade on Brophy's street. He didn't have time to turn around. Besides, he didn't want to lead them toward Brophy. He'd already done his friend a disservice by bringing them to his door.

How did they know?

The question fell away as he approached the police vehicles. Contemplation was for another day. Today was about survival.

Both drivers stood behind the open wing of their car door. Their first reaction was to fire at him. Sharp *plinks* sounded as the bullets slapped against the metal of the Jeep. A round struck the windshield, blasting a hole and spiderwebbing the safety glass.

Sandy leaned left to see through less blemished glass. He pushed the accelerator down further, nearly to the floor.

The expressions of both drivers seemed to turn to panic

simultaneously. The one on Sandy's right scrambled away from the car door toward the curb. The one on the left was between the two vehicles with nowhere to go. In desperation, he leapt into the car itself.

Sandy cranked the wheel to the left at the last possible moment, guiding the Jeep around the barricade. He let up on the gas slightly before the wheels struck the curb and hopped onto the sidewalk. Then Sandy whipped the steering wheel back to the right and punched the accelerator.

Excited shouts came through the open window as he sped down the sidewalk. Once he passed several trees and a fire hydrant, he shot between two cars parked at the curb to get back on the street.

At the first intersection, he hung a right, and sped away.

He knew he didn't have long. Those two drivers would recover and be behind him in no time.

Sandy took another turn, navigating toward a grocery store he remembered passing on the taxi ride to Brophy's house. His mind kept clicking through what he'd seen during the brief moments during the escape from Brophy's street. There'd been plenty of federal agents on the scene. They'd come equipped with their own vehicles. But something was missing.

No local police, Sandy realized.

There was no chance the Denver PD would have refused an assist. The only possibility was the Feds didn't ask for any.

That meant they were still trying to keep this quiet, at least when it came to outside the agency. He was sure it was on more than a few lips *within* the agency. What happened in Spokane was something they'd want blood for. He had no doubt of that. A wounded agent and an escaped suspect were also embarrassing for them. They wanted to recover some lost face by catching him themselves, without any outside help.

Sandy cut into an alley. He was a block away from the store

now. He glanced in the rear view mirror and saw no pursuit. No sound of sirens came through the open window. The only sound was the way the air whistled through the bullet hole in the windshield.

Was his guess right? He hoped so. If the Feds were containing this manhunt, that worked to his significant advantage.

But he couldn't rely on hope.

The grocery store was one of the mega-sized outlets. The parking lot was large enough for him to disappear into it. He slid the Jeep into a stall between a big Dodge truck and someone's mini-RV. Grabbing his small bag, he exited the vehicle. His eyes were already searching for pursuit.

He saw none.

Sandy strode purposefully through the lot until he found a late-nineties Honda Accord with the window down. He got into the driver's seat as if he owned the car. The funk of stale cigarette smoke filled his nostrils. The passenger side floor was littered with empty fast food bags.

From inside his bag, he withdrew a small screwdriver. Jamming it into the ignition, he applied enough force to snap the safety lock. The engine rumbled to life.

Sandy murmured thanks to the gods of engineering mistakes as he backed out of the parking space. He guessed he had less than half an hour before the car owner realized he'd stolen the vehicle. Add in more time for that person to navigate the police reporting system. He knew the license plate would be unofficially listed as stolen as soon as the police got the word. An official report would follow.

Stolen cars weren't a high priority. The cops wouldn't actively search for this battered old Honda. His only danger was calling attention to himself and having a nosy patrol officer investigate. That'd result in a plate check and *then* he'd be screwed.

He had time, though. Not much, but some.

Sandy followed the signs to I-25 North. He drove toward Fort Collins, a trip he figured would use up most of his time cushion where the car was concerned. No problem there. He'd ditch the car in another parking lot and hop on a bus in Fort Collins.

His mind drifted while he drove. It landed on the same question he had on Brophy's street. How had the Feds known he'd be there? Brophy's connection was to Keegan Moore, not Sandy Banks. He never told anyone in Spokane about his former life, only speaking in general terms. He never mentioned Brophy or Evan or where they'd been.

So how?

Brophy had revved his engine once before departing. One rev meant he saw nothing specific. That only meant they were too well hidden for Brophy to spot them. When had they taken up those positions? How much did they overhear? Why wait?

These questions rolled through Sandy's mind while he drove. The one he kept coming back to was the biggest one.

How had they known?

A sick feeling appeared in the pit of his stomach as a possibility sprang into his head.

Did Brophy betray me?

Sandy shook his head. He didn't believe that. He couldn't. Not after the hell they'd been through together. Not from the way his old friend reacted. He'd been ready to gun up for action.

No, it wasn't Brophy.

Sandy racked his brain. Was it Brian? He'd discovered the only other remaining horseman near the end was actually cooperating with the Feds. But what did Brian know? He'd never uttered a word about Brophy.

Or had he? Brian had been his closest relationship as a friend after Bill died and Hank retired and moved away.

They'd spent a few evenings drinking and swapping war stories. Sandy restricted his own to his police days, glossing over his military service as uneventful. Had something slipped?

What if it had? It shouldn't matter. He had no paperwork with Keegan Moore's name on it, for that matter. So how had they…?

A terrible realization sunk in.

He'd made another mistake, years ago. Before Cal came along.

The two visits.

And now Brophy was paying for it.

"Goddamn it!" Sandy slapped the steering wheel. "When does it stop?"

But he knew the answer.

It never ends.

5

Two weeks later

Agent Lori Carter struggled not to shout at her boss, Special Agent-in-Charge Edward Maw. It was difficult when everything that came out of his mouth was one hundred percent stupidity.

"I'm already working twelve hours a day on the Banks case," she said. "I can't take on additional cases."

Maw's lined face bore the innate, undeserved superiority of every middle manager Carter had ever known. "Authorization is required for any overtime, Agent Carter. I don't recall giving that authorization."

"You didn't. I've been using my own time."

"That is against policy."

"Sir, I'm trying to catch a fugitive. A man who wounded a federal agent and ended his career."

"I know very well what Banks did," snapped Maw. "I also know about your partner. I signed off on his application for disability retirement and sent it up the chain weeks ago."

"Then you know why I want—"

"What *you* want isn't an organizational priority."

Carter broke off, stunned. "Are you trying to tell me the FBI doesn't care about Banks?"

"Of course, we do. Don't be melodramatic."

"I'm not trying to be melodramatic, but—"

"But you're doing a good job of it," Maw interrupted.

She lifted her hand and dropped it. "I don't get it."

"Then allow me to explain it to you. We got good mileage out of the Spokane arrests. The role of Banks was downplayed. To the public, he's a ghost. To us, he's on our internal top ten wanted list, so—"

"Which he should be."

Maw scowled. "Don't interrupt me."

Carter clenched her jaw. There had been a glorious moment back in Spokane, when she delivered a dead detective and a corrupt police captain to Maw all in a nice bow. The power dynamic tilted in that moment, putting all of it at her end of the relationship. She ran with that shift and enjoyed its brief run. Then the situation ended and the distribution of power returned to normal. Maw had been repaying her for those few hours in the sun ever since.

All of this was unspoken between them. Maw's self-satisfied smirk was enough to bring it all rushing back to her.

"So…" he continued, "Banks will remain on that list. You will follow up on any tips or leads. In the meantime, you will return to the regular rotation in terms of new cases."

"That's a bad idea," she grumbled.

"Perhaps," he allowed. "But continuing to let you spin your wheels is a worse one. The debacle in Denver—"

"We didn't have time to get completely set up," Carter protested. "And we were understaffed for the operation."

"Excuses." Maw shook his head in disgust. "You know who makes excuses? I'll tell you who—losers. Don't make excuses. Show me results."

Carter scowled. "Keep me on the case and I will."

"Why should I? Aside from the Denver mess, you've shown me nothing for weeks. Even your supplemental reports have receded to a trickle."

"I've been holding back until I run down each lead."

"Like what? Convince me not to scale back this operation."

"What do you want to know?" Carter asked.

"Start simple. You've finished your work-up on his accomplice, correct?"

She gave him a bare nod. "I don't have enough to charge him as an accomplice, though. There's zero evidence he knew Banks was a fugitive."

"You don't believe that fairy tale, do you?"

"Of course not. But it's not what I believe, it's what I can prove. He steadfastly maintains all he got was a visit from an old friend. According to him, he was headed to the store for more beer when we stopped him."

"Awfully convenient that was the same time Banks chose to flee."

"He's lying," Carter agreed. She didn't bother to share with him Brophy already had a fridge full of beer at home. When she asked him about that, the old soldier only shrugged, and said, "You can never have too much beer."

"He confirmed Banks went by a different name," Maw said. "At least you got that much."

"It was the only helpful comment he made." She knew Brophy had no choice in the matter. If he was going to maintain his ignorance and claim all that he knew was an old army buddy stopped in to see him, he couldn't very well deny knowing that man's name. Even so, she could sense the unwillingness in Brophy to share that detail. "But he gave me Keegan Fuller. From there, I was able to access his military records."

"I've read this in your report already. Keegan Fuller died in a training accident at Fort Bragg." Maw turned up his hands. "A dead end."

"I thought so, too," Carter said. "But during the search warrant at Brophy's house, I saw something about another soldier, Evan Lloyd."

Maw's eyes narrowed. "This is new. Who is Lloyd?"

"Evan Lloyd was an otherwise unremarkable soldier who died in 1984." She gave him a knowing look. "At Fort Bragg. In a training accident."

"Same as Keegan Fuller," the SAC mused, his expression momentarily thoughtful. Carter didn't think he was necessarily smart, but he seemed cunning enough, at least in an office politics sort of way. Besides, it wasn't difficult to connect the dots when there were only two dots. "So Keegan Fuller dies on paper and becomes Sandy Banks?"

"Right."

"Did you do a background on Keegan Fuller?"

"Of course, I did."

"Why haven't I seen the report yet?"

"I'm still working on it."

"What's the update?"

"Keegan Fuller's military record is as thin as that of Sandy Banks. His personal information is even thinner. All I had to go on was a birth certificate and an address in Lexington, Tennessee."

"I thought Lexington was in Kentucky."

"Lots of Lexingtons, apparently. This one is in Tennessee and much smaller. Like eight thousand people."

Maw grunted.

"The address," Carter said, "was another dead end."

"No one there knew him?"

"Worse than that. The address itself didn't exist."

"And the birth certificate?"

"It's real. But it's part of a set."

Maw tilted his head, looking at her like a dog who just heard a sound he didn't recognize.

"It came with a death certificate," Carter explained. "Keegan Fuller died at age three of whooping cough."

Maw sat back in his chair, letting out a small sigh. "Intriguing," he admitted. "Sandy Banks, the cop-turned-vigilante assassin, used to be Keegan Fuller the soldier..." He look at her questioningly. "Who used to be...?"

"I have no idea."

Maw looked at her sharply.

"Yet," she added.

After a few moments, Maw's curiosity seemed to ebb. "Well, who he was twenty-five years ago doesn't matter. Catching him now does. What headway have you made toward *that?*"

"There are no burial records for Keegan Fuller. The soldier, not the child. His military jacket states 'remains released to family' but the name of the family member isn't typed into the appropriate block and the signature is illegible."

"Because there was no family," Maw concluded.

Carter nodded. "As best as I can tell, Evan Lloyd was a real person and Evan was his real name. I located the cemetery where he is buried."

Maw's expression flickered. She thought he might have seemed impressed for a moment. Then the usual officious, pinched look returned. "Where?"

"Minneapolis. I've got surveillance cameras on site."

"Who is monitoring them?"

"My CI."

Maw frowned. "Another expense outliving its usefulness," he muttered. "Don't you think it's high time Mr. Moore start serving his sentence?"

"If he wasn't a trained police officer, I'd agree. But he *is* still useful to me."

Maw sat back in his chair, steepling his fingers and striking what Carter thought of as his "look how contemplative and smart I am" pose. She waited while he played out the charade, keeping her own expression neutral. She had no intention of giving up on finding Banks. If he pulled her off the case and put her back in the rotation, her days were suddenly going to get a whole lot longer.

"I'll give you another month," Maw said.

Carter was surprised at how intensely the sense of relief rushed through her. "Thank you, sir."

"But your supplementals need to pick up," he added. "No holding onto information. I want data in real time."

She nodded that she understood.

Maw waved toward the door. "That's all, then. You're dismissed, Agent Carter."

Brian Moore greeted her with as much enthusiasm as Maw had earlier.

"Did you at least bring coffee?" he asked.

She shook her head. "A little late in the day for me."

Moore waved his hands in the air. "Great. Well, I'm out, so…"

"I'll stop at the store."

"Which does me no good right now."

Carter squinted at him. "Maybe you'd prefer a prison cell?"

Moore scoffed. He waved his hands again, this time toward the mass of screens on the nearby desk in the corner of the small, two-room apartment. "I'm already in prison," he complained. "I spend twelve hours a day staring at those screens, watching for someone who is never going to show up. I eat, sleep for a while, get up and fast forward through the hours I missed. Then I stare at the screen some more."

"You eat good food and sleep on a comfortable bed," Carter said. "Don't forget that."

Moore leveled a finger at her. "This should count against my sentence."

"This is the reason your sentence isn't life, Brian. So, get a grip."

Moore crossed his arms and looked away.

"Anything to report?" Carter asked him.

"No," he answered brusquely. "There's never anything to report. That's the point. My eyes are burning out of my head and I'm going stir crazy, all for nothing."

"I repeat, would you prefer a prison cell?"

Moore sighed and rubbed his arms before dropping them to his sides. "Honestly, at this point, I don't even know."

Carter changed the subject. "Does the name Keegan Fuller mean anything to you?"

Moore shook his head dully.

"How about Evan Lloyd?"

"Other than being the name on the gravestone on camera? Nope."

"And Janet?"

Moore turned his gaze to her. "You've already asked me that, too. Are you trying to trick me or something?"

"How can I trick you if you're telling the truth?"

"You can't," Moore insisted. "Because I am. Jesus, I already betrayed my friend. I told you everything. I'm Judas, all right? Collecting my thirty pieces of silver and everything. I'm all-in."

Carter examined him carefully. Then she nodded. "All right." She motioned toward the screens on the desk. "Keep watching. I'll go buy some coffee."

On the way to the store, she made a decision. Maybe Banks wasn't going to be on the official top ten most wanted list, with his likeness emblazoned on the FBI website, but she was done keeping his status completely dark.

She called the records division and spoke to Ted, who seemed like he'd been in that office for eighty years. "The fugitive warrant on Banks?" she said. "Go ahead and enter it into NCIC."

"You got it," Ted said easily.

At her direction, he'd been holding onto a signed arrest warrant since the day after everything went to hell in Spokane. Keeping it out of the system was actually at Maw's insistence. It was one of the first places he reasserted his authority after the arrest of Captain Valczinski.

"Let's clean up our own mess, shall we?" he sneered at her.

Carter went along with it. She wanted to be the one to bring Banks in, especially since he wounded Scott. But she was running out of time and past worrying about who got credit. With a fugitive warrant in the system, at least there was some small chance a local cop might come across him and put him in cuffs.

"It's done," Ted told her.

"That was quick."

"I had it in the queue," he explained. "I just needed to enter the date of issue and it was ready to go. Do you want me to send it out as an alert?"

"No," she said. That would cue Maw to what she'd done. He'd already be royally pissed if he discovered she'd countermanded his order. But if some officer or deputy somewhere managed to stumble across Banks and lasso him in for them, the SAC wouldn't care much about how it happened at that point. It was a calculated roll of the dice. "Thanks, Ted," she said.

"Anytime."

They hung up.

Carter scrolled through her contacts, glancing down from the road ahead while she drove. When she found Mark Szoke, she pressed CALL.

Szoke answered on the third ring. "Hey, Lori. You calling to say you're coming back to me?"

"Very funny." They'd gone on two dates, discovered their chemistry wasn't of the romantic kind, and remained friends. Even so, Szoke never seemed to tire of the joke.

"Where are you?" he asked.

"Just outside Alexandria," she said. "You?"

"Not close enough for dinner," he said. "So, what's up?"

"I need some help with something."

"Wait. This is an historic moment. The FBI... and for those of you playing at home, that's the Federal Bureau of Investigation, the mighty bastion of justice spearheaded by J. Edgar—"

"Stop."

"—Hoover himself," Szoke continued, "is asking the lowly CIA for help?"

"Yes."

"You need your dry cleaning picked up?"

"No. I'm serious here."

"Oh." Szoke paused. "Is this a clean line?"

"It's my bureau phone."

"Then probably not."

"You want to meet instead?"

"I wish I could. But, like I said, I'm away."

"How far?"

Szoke didn't answer for a few seconds. Finally, he said, "Go ahead and give it to me now. I'll see what I can do. What is it?"

Now Carter paused, considering how best to frame her question. She decided Szoke needed some context if he was going to get to what she needed.

"I'm looking for a fugitive named Sandy Banks," she began, and then told him everything.

6

1982

He packed lunch for two early that morning. Then he made an extra sandwich for his breakfast and slipped out before his mother or step-father awoke. His fishing gear was in the small wooden shed his father built years ago. He grabbed what he needed and started toward his favorite spot, munching the peanut butter and jelly as he strode along.

He walked down the road for a while, then took a wide pathway into the woods. Ash trees and poplars dotted the landscape and slowly closed in on him. He found the game trail and followed it. Before long, he was there.

Once he settled into the familiar spot, his back against a tree, he tossed in his line. It was slightly chilly but he knew it would warm up as the day passed. He concentrated on the end of his pole for a long while, pushing everything out of his mind. When that grew too difficult, he took a book from his backpack and started reading. The letters jumbled on the page, made for slow going, but he stuck with it. The story about the battle between rival teenage social classes in Tulsa drew him in. So much, in fact, he didn't hear her approach until she was almost upon him.

"Hey!" she called.

He looked up to see her smiling his way. He smiled and lowered the book. "Hey," he called back.

Janet reached his location and plopped down next to him. "Whew. Chores took forever."

"Mine will be waiting for me when I get home."

"Always putting everything off. That's you, William Sutter."

"Not everything," he said, and kissed her.

She kissed him back, tentatively at first, then more eagerly. After a while, she broke away and fanned herself with her hand. "Whew," she said again. "That was certainly worth the walk."

He felt the same way, of course, and so he grinned like an idiot. A lightness played in his chest.

She laughed and pushed his shoulder. "Why are you looking at me like that?"

"Because I love you."

Janet tilted her head. "Well, I love you, too."

They stared at each other for a few seconds. Then Janet giggled and glanced away. When she looked back and found him still staring, she leaned forward and gave him a quick kiss on the mouth. "Come on," she said, standing up.

He stood with her. "Where to?"

She jerked her head toward the edge of the creek only a few steps away, already moving that direction.

He followed.

Janet sat on the sandy bank and pulled her shoes off. Then

she dipped her feet into the water. He joined her there.

"You'll scare off the fish," he teased.

"With my stinky feet, you mean?" she teased back. "It's not like they're biting, anyway, are they?"

"No," he admitted. He peeled off his own boots and rolled up his pants. Then he sat beside her and slipped his feet into the water.

Janet kicked her legs gently in the light current of Sugar Creek. She reached out and took his hand. They sat, holding hands for a long while. He could hear the water flowing past, the birds chirping, and her occasional exhale.

"I think this is just about my favorite place in the whole wide world," she said reverently.

"Why?" he asked.

"It's so quiet. So beautiful. So… untouched by the rest of the world."

He thought about her words, and agreed. "It's mine, too," he said.

"Oh, yeah?" She turned his own question back on him. "Why?"

He considered his answer. Being in this place did somehow feel… *apart* from all of the other aspects of his life. Especially the hard parts. His father's death. Errol's temper. He didn't exactly forget while he was here. They just seemed more *distant*.

And that was a welcome respite.

He knew he could tell her all of that. She already knew most of it and would understand the rest. Instead, he just smiled at her again. "Because you're here."

She smiled back and leaned sideways, nudging his shoulder with her own. "Sweet talker."

"Might be sweet, but it's also true."

"Might be that's what makes it sweet."

"I expect so."

They sat quietly some more. Then she said, in a quieter tone, "I always want to feel this way."

"Me, too."

"I mean it," she said earnestly. "I don't want to be like all those other people, all those grownups who… I don't know. Either they never felt like this or they lost it somehow." She thought for a second, then shrugged. "I don't know which is worse."

"Losing it is worse," he said.

"Maybe." She pointed, keeping her voice low. "See there?"

He followed her finger. A small frog had climbed up a branch poking out of the water. He watched the creature for a few moments. Then he closed his free hand around hers. She turned to face him, so he kissed her again, this time slowly. When he pulled away, she didn't move, but kept her eyes closed. Then they fluttered open and she smiled.

"We could promise," she said. "Swear forever?"

He nodded immediately. "Yes," he agreed.

"Okay," she said. "By the power of the frog vested in me…"

He laughed and pushed at her shoulder gently. "I thought you were serious."

"I am totally serious," she said, her smile playful. He caught a hint of seriousness in her tone, too. "If we can get through the next year, it'll all be easy from there."

He supposed she was right. Finish this last year of high school. One last year living under Errol. Then he and Janet could go anywhere. Get a car and leave Big Sandy behind forever. Hell, they didn't even have to stay in Tennessee. He didn't care where he was, if it meant he could be with her.

"I swear," he whispered.

"Me, too," she whispered back.

They let those words hang in the air as they sat, dipping their feet into Sugar Creek, the promise of the rest of the day together still before them.

7

2011
Four months after Denver

Sandy stroked the side of Gopher's neck while the horse snuf-fled at his palm with her lips, gingerly drawing the slice of apple into her mouth. She raised her head and chewed.

"Atta girl," Sandy said, patting the sorrel. "Don't tell Hank, though, huh?"

He smiled at Gopher's guileless expression.

"You just want more apple," he said. "You don't care who knows it."

Gopher finished chewing and nosed around Sandy's hands and clothing inquisitively.

"That's all I had," said Sandy.

He gave her a final pat and glanced around the barn, making sure he'd taken care of everything. Satisfied his work was done, he headed to the door and trudged toward the main house. The wide open expanse of Montana sky was spread out above him. He breathed in the cold, clear air wistfully. He knew his time here was almost over.

Inside the house, he took off his boots in the mud room. He knocked the dirt off of them before slipping on some moccasins. Then he went the rest of the way inside. The warmth of the interior washed over him, thanks to the crackling fire in the living room. He spotted Hank's stocking feet resting on the footrest of his ancient Barcalounger as he padded into the kitchen. There, he found the coffee pot still half full. Grateful, he poured a cup and joined Hank in the living room.

"Horses are in," he told his host.

"Good," Hank said. "Going to be a cold one. Summer's definitely over."

Sandy could hear the rasp of age in his voice, something that hadn't been there when his former partner left Spokane years ago.

Time catches us all.

Sandy settled into the other chair in the small living room. He sipped his coffee and watched the flames dance. After a few minutes passed, he said, "I think it's time for me to move on."

Hank didn't seemed surprised. "I figured that was coming."

"You did, huh?"

"Yeah. 'Course, the day bag sitting on your bed was a bit of a clue."

Sandy smiled slightly. He didn't feel like Hank was being nosy. The house wasn't big, and he left the door to the guest room open. The small bag contained a change of clothes, identification paperwork, some cash, his .45, and a sap. The leather sap was a gift from Cal. The old-school police tool was about as long as a hunting knife and shaped like a flattened, miniature baseball bat. The fat end was filled with sand. When swung with force, the blow packed a wallop. Sandy was pretty certain the item was no longer legal, even back when Cal gave it to him. It certainly wasn't approved for police use.

"You know," said Hank, "for a guy who hardly ever left home, you always had something restless about you, Sandy."

"You're the one that left the team," Sandy reminded him. He waved his hand at his surroundings. "Came out here, three quarters of the way off the grid."

Hank grunted. "Like to drop that last one quarter part, if I could."

Sandy didn't answer. When Hank left The Horsemen, he cited not wanting to lie to his wife any longer. Sandy thought it was a good reason, even if it didn't matter much in the end.

"Goddamn government," grumbled Hank, "should mind its own goddamned business."

Since it was that very government pursuing him, Sandy tended to agree with the sentiment. "I appreciate what you've done for me here," he said to Hank. "Giving me a place to lay low."

Hank had done more than that, Sandy knew. He'd given him some purpose during these last few months of hiding. Meaningful work to do. He'd paid Sandy in cash which he supposed helped both of them.

"You're welcome to stay through the winter," Hank said. "Or longer."

"I appreciate the offer."

"I mean it. You're a good hand and I ain't getting any younger." Hank shrugged. "Not only that, but you've been good company. It's been quiet here since Belinda passed."

"I know."

"Plus…" Hank trailed off.

"Plus what?"

Hank shrugged again. "Look, when I left Spokane, every-thing changed. I liquidated everything. I even sold my pension to one of those companies that buys annuities." He grunted. "Fucking vultures, but I got my lump sum, along with all the other assets we sold."

"And you changed your name," Sandy said.

"That was the easy part. I put that in place years before I made the move. Had to give Henry Cartwright a little bit of history."

"Makes sense."

"I got away clean," Hank said. "Nothing but another social security number to the Feds and a lot number to the county. As long as I pay the goddamn taxes to both every year, they leave me alone."

"A perfect escape," said Sandy. "I always wondered how you did it. At least, until I got your letter."

"You burned it, right?" Hank asked.

"For the tenth time, yes."

"I just want to be sure."

"What I can't figure out is why you risked sending it in the first place."

Hank looked away, staring into the fire. "That's what I'm trying to tell you. It's not just that it's been good to have someone around again. It has, but it's more than that. Something I didn't expect."

Sandy watched him, listening.

Hank reached up and removed his glasses. He rubbed his eyes with the other. "Leaving that old life behind made sense at the time. Hell, it still does. Aside from Belinda, there was no family to worry about. Nothing to miss. And for those first couple of years, I didn't miss any of it at all." He stopped rubbing his eyes and replaced his glasses. "Then I lost Belinda. After the grief faded a little, I was left with this… overwhelming loneliness. You know what I mean?"

Sandy did know. That loneliness made up the bulk of his life.

"It's not like I'm going to drive my truck into town and make new friends at the feed store. I keep a low profile for a reason—it's safer. Even if I did become friendly with some of those town folks…" He looked over at Sandy again. "Well, it's not like they can ever really know me."

Sandy nodded slowly. "Hank, I've lived that way almost my entire life."

"Then you understand."

"I think so."

"Belinda… she knew and understood me in a way no other human being ever will. But it's been good to have you here, Sandy. Good to… well, good to be *known*, I guess."

"Likewise," Sandy said. "But I can't stay. They're looking for me."

"I know that. This is a good place to hide. They won't find you here. If they do…" Hank tapped the .45 at hip. "We'll Ruby Ridge the shit out of them."

"I'd like to avoid that."

Hank grunted. "The older I get, the less I care. Might be a good way to go."

Sandy didn't answer.

After a while, Hank said, "Well, you're in good shape to keep under the radar. Your hair, the beard, the cash you've earned…"

On reflex, Sandy reached up to his hair. He'd dyed it a muddy brown and let it grow. His bushy beard only added to the new look, one he hoped would escape casual interest from anyone hunting for him.

Hank fell silent again. Sandy let the silence sit for a while. Both men drank their coffee and stared into the fire. For his part, Sandy was mildly surprised at how open Hank had been. The gruff, older man had never seemed to him like a person who spent time contemplating. Then again, he supposed everyone had thoughts and feelings they didn't actually say.

Which led him to his gratitude once more. Hank had taken a chance on him. Three times, in fact. Once to send him the letter detailing how to find him in Montana. He'd been vague, forcing Sandy to crack the cipher he was using, but it wasn't exactly the Enigma code. The FBI analysts would have been able to figure it out if they got their hands on the letter. That would never happen now, though. Sandy had shredded and then burnt it once he committed the information to memory.

That brought on the second risk. Sandy put together a small package and mailed it to Hank. Generic return address. No fingerprints anywhere on the paper. Just an unassuming packet containing some cash and a few important documents in the name of Matthew Creighton with Sandy's photo on all of them.

His out, if he ever needed it.

Sheltering Sandy for the past several months was the largest of the three risks Hank took on his behalf. Sandy was nearly certain he'd slipped any pursuit after leaving Colorado. But *nearly* isn't *absolutely*. It was possible he could have led the Feds right to Hank's doorstep. Then Agent Carter and her cohorts would not only have Sandy but the only other Horseman who remained outstanding.

Thankfully, it didn't happen that way. If the Feds knew he was here, they would have made a move long ago. He was safe here. He could probably remain safe here for the rest of his days, like he knew Hank would.

But there was something he needed to do.

And Hank deserved to know what it was.

"It's not just the risk of the Feds finding you because of me," Sandy said, still gazing into the flames. "There's another reason I need to go."

"Let me guess—a woman."

Sandy turned to him, once more surprised. First Brophy

guessed, now Hank. Was he that obvious? "Yes. How'd you know?"

Hank lifted his chin and scratched behind his own beard. "It's always a woman. Who is she?"

"She's…" Sandy paused, suddenly cautious about saying her name. It wasn't that he didn't trust Hank. If he didn't know who she was, he couldn't tell anyone, no matter how much pressure was exerted upon him. "She's someone I loved. A long time ago."

Hank let out another one of his knowing grunts. Sandy had grown accustomed to the sound over the past months. "But you left her?"

"I had no choice."

"There's always a choice."

Sandy shook his head, thinking back to those dark days of his youth. "Not always," he said quietly.

Hank thought that over. Then he said, "You said it was a long time ago?"

Sandy nodded.

"Probably she's moved on," Hank said. "Especially if you broke her heart."

"I had to leave," Sandy said. "But I said goodbye. She made me promise to come back to her."

He remembered those brief, painful moments. The aching loss followed him for years. So, too, did Janet's clear eyes, filled with resolute love, beseeching him.

You come back to me, she'd said.

"So, now I will," Sandy said, speaking more to Janet's memory than to the man across from him. "Maybe she'll refuse to see me. Or curse me. Maybe she has a life that doesn't have any room for me in it. But maybe…"

He shrugged.

"The only way to know is to go to her and see."

Hank didn't argue. The older man was silent for a while.

When he spoke again, he asked one of the two questions that had been hounding Sandy since he fled from Spokane.

"You think you can find her?"

"Yes," he said, without hesitation. It was the easier of the two questions to answer. Sandy waited for the other, more difficult one to come.

But Hank didn't ask it. Instead, he spoke in a resigned tone.

"Well, I guess you have to go then, don't you?" He glanced over at Sandy. "If she's your Belinda, you can't let that go."

8

Sandy rose early the next morning. He took the time to feed the animals and make coffee before he finished packing his meager belongings.

When he walked into the kitchen, Hank stood at the stove, cooking breakfast. He was nearly done. Several strips of bacon sat atop the finished hash browns while he monitored the eggs closely.

"Still going, are ya?" the old man asked.

"Why wouldn't I be?"

"Quite a few reasons," said Hank. "If you've thought it through at all, you'd see that."

Sandy *had* thought it through. He knew Hank was right about those reasons. He had a good situation here, almost entirely off the grid. Safe. Going back out into the world risked being caught. His dyed, longer hair and beard weren't a foolproof disguise.

But he doubted that was all Hank meant. There was Janet, too. Could he find her? Was he putting her at risk if he did?

The idea had haunted him for the last few months. But he knew he'd never told anyone about Janet. There was no connection between her and Sandy Banks. Nor between her and Keegan Fuller, the name he'd carried while in the Army. Sure, Brophy and Evan had known he had a girl back home, but he'd never said her name or where home was.

There was no connection.

As long as he wasn't being actively followed when he found her, there was no danger.

That wasn't all, though, was it?

Years had passed. Twenty-seven of them. He'd counted them up in his head and then brooded on the number. Almost three decades.

What if she has a life?

It wasn't an *if*, he realized. She had a life. He knew it. Everyone did. The bigger questions were, was it a life she was happy with and one she deserved?

Almost certainly, yes.

But what if it wasn't?

He knew it took a special breed of arrogance to think he might be the answer to that. That he could be what could make her happy if she wasn't already. Then he thought back to that promise they made on the banks of Sugar Creek, all those years ago. He remembered her last words to him, less than a year later, before he fled Big Sandy and became Keegan Fuller.

"You come back to me."

Of course, she'd been an eighteen year old girl then. She'd be a forty-five year old woman now. Probably living a full, happy life, not having thought of him for years.

But he still loved her. He made a promise. So he had to find out.

Otherwise, what was the point of it all? His whole life has

been about violence and, even if finding her came to nothing in the end, he needed to see her one last time.

To know.

He didn't say any of that to Hank. He guessed the old man understood it anyway.

Hank pricked the egg yolk slightly with the corner of his spatula. Dark yellow flowed out. Then he scooped some of the hot grease and dribbled it over the top, cauterizing the wound. He repeated the process with the other egg. To Sandy, it looked like two yellow eyes weeping.

"I like to call this eggs high chaparral," Hank said. "Grab a couple of plates, will you? Let's get a good meal in your belly before you go."

9

Three days later

It was a risk, he knew. But everything he did these days was a risk. And Minneapolis *was* on the way to Tennessee.

Mostly.

Sandy came into the better known twin city already not feeling well. The cough that hit him before he was even out of Montana had worsened. He spent one night in a motel in North Dakota, hacking up phlegm and shivering beneath the thin blankets. Now, as he left the bus station, he felt warm and somewhat spacey. The sensation was strangely peaceful.

Going to Evan's grave wasn't smart. He knew that. Despite the danger, he wanted to pay his respects. In all the time he lived in Spokane, he'd never made the trip, so a sense of duty drove him. Besides, he reasoned, the Feds may not even be aware of Evan's existence or any connection to his Keegan Fuller identity. And if they did know, so what? He'd been off the grid for four months. If they were willing to stake out a grave, they'd never keep at it for that long.

If anything, Sandy was willing to bet his case had come off the front burner and been slid to the back one. He hadn't been in federal law enforcement but, in his own experience, bosses were only willing to expend time and money toward a case for so long. Something new, shiny and demanding was always coming along behind, clamoring for attention.

Then again, he *had* shot and wounded a federal agent. That probably merited some extra time on that front burner.

He stopped at a bookstore and bought a city map. The cemetery was on the edge of town, so Sandy took a cab. At his request, the driver let him off at the entrance. A pair of black, wrought-iron gates stood wide open. Sandy walked through them and found an information station just inside. It only took a few seconds to get the location of Evan's grave and to examine the wall map for the cemetery layout.

Sandy walked slowly toward his destination, his senses now on high alert. Traffic inside the cemetery was minimal. He saw a couple of men in their sixties standing near one head-stone, one consoling the other while he wept. A grounds-keeper whizzed past Sandy on a golf cart. Other than that, the place seemed empty.

As he drew near, he stopped and took a seat on a bench. There, he sat for a long while, paying attention to his sur-roundings. He detected no one hiding. None of the admit-tedly few people he saw going about their business seemed to act out of the ordinary.

His danger radar did not ping.

Sandy sniffed and wiped his nose, shivering suddenly. Then he rose and walked the rest of the way to Evan's grave.

The stone was simple. So was the inscription. Just his name and the inscription *beloved son*. Those two words cut into him. He envisioned Evan's parents standing where he was now. He couldn't imagine the pain they'd felt. Their son had gone away to serve his country. He'd returned home to be buried. His parents were told a vague story about a training accident and given a small death benefit. Then the government moved on and forgot about all of it.

He doubted Evan's mother and father forgot. The Army lost a soldier. They lost a son.

And it was my fault.

Sandy swallowed hard. His eyes prickled with tears he refused to let fall. He knew he was being selfish in a way, taking the blame onto himself. Some of it lay elsewhere. Maybe most of it. None of that would have mattered if he'd done his part. If he'd made different decisions, and taken different actions.

He wanted to ask Evan for forgiveness. But he couldn't bring the words up to his lips, and he doubted there'd be any reply from the cold, hard stone.

So, he stood there, his hands thrust in his pockets, feeling the flush of a fever growing inside him, and not caring. Maybe it was some sort of penance. One last burden he could bear in order to come a little closer to bringing the scales back to even.

Not that he ever could.

The cold seeped into him as he stood nearly still next to the headstone. He began to shiver after a while. He tried to work up the will to at least say he was sorry, but even that felt like he was getting off too easily. So Sandy merely pressed his lips together, his eyes locked on the etched letters of Evan's name, and nodded a few times. Then he took a deep breath and turned away.

As he strode toward the open gate of the cemetery, he half-expected a black helicopter to swoop in, along with a half dozen SUVs and vans full of men in black fatigues. Instead, all he got was a casual, two-fingered salute from the grounds-keeper as the man rolled past on his cart.

Sandy left the cemetery.

10

Carter's phone buzzed. She was doing an Internet search for Keegan Fuller for the umpteenth time, tweaking the request each time and hoping for some sort of a digital trail that led backward to whoever Sandy Banks/Keegan Fuller *really* was.

She lifted the phone and saw it was Moore. She hit the connection button. "Carter."

"Holy shit," said Moore excitedly. "It's him. At least, I think it's him."

Carter sat up straight, immediately attentive. "Banks?"

"Yeah, I think so. Same build, at least."

"He was at the cemetery?"

"Yeah. At the grave, just like you thought he would be." Moore's voice was ringed with excitement. "Holy shit," he repeated.

"Are you sure it was him?"

"No," Moore admitted. "I mean, the camera's not great. And it looks like he was wearing a disguise. A fake beard, a wig, and a hat. Either that or he grew his hair out."

"But he stood right at the gravestone? *The* gravestone?"

"Two feet away from Evan Lloyd's headstone, yes."

"Is he still there?"

"No. I was making lunch, so I missed it live. When I did a review, I found it. He stood there for about fifteen minutes and—"

"What's the time delay?"

"Twenty-two minutes," Moore reported.

"Give me a description."

Moore rattled off the nondescript clothing. "The hat is dark-colored, no insignia," he added.

"Got it," said Carter.

She hung up without saying goodbye. A quick search resulted in the number for the Minneapolis office. She selected it and pressed send.

While the phone rang in her ear, she looked down at her right hand. Her fingers trembled with excitement.

I'm going to catch you this time.

11

Sandy entered the bus station, glad for the comparative warmth it offered. The Minnesota fall was somehow colder than he was used to in Spokane. The fact he was sick might be skewing his perception, of course. It didn't matter. All he wanted to do right now was get a ticket to Milwaukee. There, he'd hole up in a motel for a couple of days until he felt better.

Then he'd go home.

Tennessee.

Aside from wanting to be well when he arrived, stopping off in Milwaukee served another purpose. He might still be flying way under the radar, but it was still safer not to go directly to his final destination.

They don't know about home, he thought.

They don't know about Janet.

Even so, years of caution drove his decisions.

He threaded his way through the crowd toward the ticket

counters. Two counters were open. The lines at both were only a half-dozen deep. Sandy chose one and looked up at the massive scheduling board. Under Departures, he located Milwaukee. He was in luck. The next bus left in forty minutes.

"Sir?"

The voice came from behind him and to the left. Sandy craned his neck around to see a uniformed officer several feet away. For a second, he thought the man might be security. The powder blue color of the shirt was one favored by security companies on the west coast since most agencies opted for the LAPD black for their uniforms. Then he noticed the gun at the man's hip. Sandy's gaze flicked to the badge, still hoping for armed security or even transit police. Both tended to receive less training than—

Minneapolis Police Department, engraved on the badge.

"Yes?" Sandy answered, forcing his expression to what he hoped resembled a confused and slightly concerned civilian.

The officer, a fit black man with a well-trimmed mustache, gave him a slight wave. "Can we talk to you for a moment?"

We?

Sandy's head swiveled further. He spotted another cop behind him, this one angled from his right. He was white and built like a bull. His flat expression betrayed nothing. The pair had triangulated him in their approach. Such a tactic might have been automatic for a veteran, well-trained patrol officer. It also told Sandy something else.

They expected trouble.

"Is there a problem?" he asked.

"No, sir. We just want to speak with you for a minute."

Sandy motioned toward the ticket counter. "I don't want to lose my place in line."

"You'll get it back," the officer promised.

"All right," Sandy agreed amiably.

In his peripheral vision, he scanned for more police. Was

it just these two or was there an entire team? In that moment, he was grateful for the powder blue uniform shirts—they'd be easier to spot in a crowd.

The threesome walked a short distance away from the ticket counters. A long wooden bench lined the nearby wall, but it was currently empty. That seemed to be their destination. Sandy noted two exits. The front entrance where he'd come into the bus station was the furthest away. An emergency exit stood at the end of the wooden bench.

All he had to do was get there.

The two officers maintained their relative positions behind him, both a short stride away. Sandy kept his hands in plain view. He knew if he reached into a pocket or toward his belt line, things would jump off immediately. These two men knew what their plan was. His only advantage was they weren't aware that he knew.

Sandy reconsidered. Maybe they *weren't* sure who he was. This could be a pair of hardworking, diligent cops checking out anyone suspicious.

Why are they so diligent?

How could they know I was here?

He didn't have time to work that out. His time was almost up. He needed a plan of action.

"This is good," said the first officer, just a few steps away from the bench.

Sandy stopped. He gave the officer an expectant, concerned look. "What's this about?"

"Do you have some identification, sir?"

"I do, but are you going to tell me—"

"Let's take a look at that ID and then we'll talk." The politeness in his tone had a hard edge underneath.

Sandy raised his hands, placating. "No problem. Just asking." He decided not to push the matter. He needed these two less suspicious, not more. "I just don't understand what—" he said while his hand casually snaked toward his back pocket.

He hoped the words would distract them, even a little. But both men keyed on his right hand as he reached.

Sandy lifted his left hand, wriggling his fingers. "—this is all about," he said.

The first cop's eyes shifted to his left hand.

Sandy grasped the sap in his pocket and ripped it out. He stepped forward and swung at the silent cop, whose gaze had never left Sandy's hand. Too late, the officer saw the danger coming and tried to draw his weapon. Before he could clear leather, the sap clapped into his jaw. The force of the blow caused his knees to buckle. His arms dropped to his side and the big bull of a man collapsed downward like a bag of cement.

Without pause, Sandy whirled to the first officer. As he turned, he saw the man's gun coming up. Sandy chopped down viciously. The sap landed with a sharp *thunk* on the officer's forearm. A piercing cry of pain erupted from his mouth as he clutched at his arm with his opposite hand. The gun clattered harmlessly to the floor.

Sandy shuffled forward slightly, closing distance. He swept out his foot forcefully and caught the unsuspecting officer still staring down at his injured forearm. The man toppled to the ground with a surprised grunt.

Sandy didn't hesitate.

He dropped the sap and ran for the exit.

The sign on the door boldly warned exiting through it would trigger an alarm. Sandy shoved the push bar hard, popping the door outward. The promised alarm didn't sound. Sandy powered through the opening and found himself in a wide alley. He turned left, away from the front of the bus station and ran.

His mind clicked through options even as he drew air into his congested lungs. The two officers were unlikely to give chase. He suspected one had a broken bone in his forearm.

The other was unconscious at most or, at least, suffering from a concussion.

But they had radios.

And there were witnesses.

Sandy pulled the blue ball cap from his head and flung it into a dumpster as he ran. He thought about shedding his jacket as well, but the cold air convinced him otherwise. No, his best allies now were distance and blending.

He ran the first two blocks, then took a left. He dropped into a power walk for another block, then slowed to a speed he hoped would blend better with other pedestrians. Those other civilians had eyed him strangely while he ran, but now no one gave him a second glance.

Several blocks away, a siren erupted, followed by another. Suddenly, a third howled from just up the street, accompanied by the throaty roar of a car engine. A black and white marked SUV police vehicle hurtled in his direction.

Sandy ducked into a small grocery store.

The police car whipped past, headed toward the bus station.

He watched it go. Adrenaline surged in his veins. It was official—he was on the run again. Like in Spokane.

Sandy opened the door to the grocery store and exited. He lowered his head and hurried in the opposite direction the police car had gone. As he strode quickly down the sidewalk, a terrible sense of familiarity came over him.

Being on the run didn't only happen in Spokane.

No, it seemed like he'd always been running, his whole life.

12

"Lori?"

Agent Lori Carter was reaching for the door handle to her car when the voice came from the shadows behind a round pillar in the parking garage. She whirled around, reaching for her weapon and dropping into a combat stance.

Mark Szoke stepped forward, his hands raised in a calming gesture. "Easy, it's just me."

Carter let go of the pistol grip and stood straight up again. "What are you doing here? I thought you were…" She stopped, realizing he'd never said. "Too far away to get dinner," she finished instead.

"I was. I'm back now. You know how it is."

She nodded, though she didn't have an entirely clear idea. The FBI involved more travel than some law enforcement agencies, but the Marshals had it way worse. As for the CIA, Carter guessed it ranged from desk-bound analysts to globe-hopping field agents like Szoke.

Then another thought struck her.

"Why are you *here*, though? The company doesn't have any offices in this building."

"No," Szoke admitted. "I came to see you."

"That's great," Carter said, "but I don't have time to socialize. Minneapolis police just encountered my fugitive. I'm catching a flight up there to coordinate."

"I know."

She tilted her head. "You *know?*"

"We need to talk," Szoke said.

Carter shook her head. "I don't have time. My flight leaves in—"

"I have a company jet waiting at Hyde Field," Szoke said. "I'll take you there after we talk." He glanced at his watch. "You'll get to Minneapolis even sooner this way."

Carter stared at him, curiosity and suspicion bubbling up. "What's going on?"

Szoke hesitated. He glanced around to see if anyone was near, but the entire level appeared empty. Then he glanced at his watch again. "There's… an interest in your fugitive."

"From who?"

"Certain individuals."

"Could you be more vague, Mark?"

"Hey, you know how intelligence works. We compartmentalize on a need-to-know basis."

"Since he's *my* fugitive," Carter growled, "don't you think I need to know?"

"That's not up to me."

"This is bullshit." She reached for the door handle to her car. "I have work to do."

"Wait," Szoke said, stepping closer. "There's more to the situation than just your case."

"I know," Carter said.

It was Szoke's turn to appear perplexed. "*What* do you know?"

"I'm not some Nancy Drew wannabe here, Mark. I've been investigating cases for a long time. I know how to dredge up facts."

Szoke frowned and held up his finger. "What facts?" he demanded. "Specifically."

"So I'm supposed to share with you but you won't reciprocate?" She shook her head. "I don't play those games."

"You tell me what you know and I'll tell you everything I know," Szoke said.

She paused, peering closely at Szoke's expression, trying to gauge his sincerity. "If I agree and you screw me, Mark…"

"I won't. Now, tell me what you know."

Carter hesitated. Then she took a breath and said, "Well, I know his DD214 is false. Sandy Banks is a creation. It's a made-up identity."

"Made-up? The guy was a cop in Spokane for twelve years."

"Under a false identity," Carter said. "He spent another twelve years after that murdering people. Nice sort of harmonic balance there, don't you think?"

"Murder might be a strong word."

"What would you call it?"

"Extra-legal justice?"

Carter snorted. "I don't know what kind of law you Langley boys operate under, but vigilante execution is still murder in my book."

"From what I read, the people he killed were piece-of-shit criminals. Worst of the worst."

Carter spread her hands. "Are we really going to have this discussion? Sure, the victims were all terrible people who got away with crimes they probably committed. But the system said they were innocent."

"The system wrongly convicts people sometimes," Szoke said. "We set that right when we discover our mistake. This is kind of like that."

"No, Mark, it isn't *kind of like that*. It's murder." She stared at him, incredulous. "Are your ethics really this flexible?"

He gave her an even stare. "Probably not. But there's an argument to be made."

"A lousy argument. Besides, it doesn't matter. He killed an innocent civilian. Kelly Merchant. And he shot a federal agent. Ended his career." She jerked a thumb toward her chest. "My partner."

"I get that." Szoke glanced at his watch. "You sure you're not taking this too personally? That it hasn't gone from a case to a crusade?"

Carter's jaw dropped. When she recovered, she said, "What is with you? Why'd you come here?"

"Because I know you. I want to help."

"I asked you for help months ago. It's been radio silence since then."

"I've been busy."

"Thanks for serving up the most common, lamest excuse ever, Mark." She crossed her arms. "Look, I need better information to figure out who this guy really is. That's the key to figuring out where he might go."

"Okay."

"So… who is he?"

"I don't know," Szoke told her. "But I think you're right about the fake DD-214."

"No shit," Carter said dismissively. "I've tracked back further than that. Keegan Fuller is the name he served under."

Genuine surprise crossed Szoke's face. "You found that, huh?"

"Yeah, asshole, I found that. I found out he supposedly died in a training accident in 1983, too. Of course, that was after he already died of whooping cough at age three."

"That's impressive," Szoke said.

"Are you going to tell me the rest?"

Szoke paused. "You know, there's something I learned early on in my career—"

"I'm not looking for folksy advice," Carter snapped. "Just tell me what you know."

"It's not advice," said Szoke. "Just something I learned. And it's pertinent."

Carter tilted her head and said nothing. It was clear he wasn't going to say any more until he got to drop his little nugget of wisdom. So, she waited.

"What I learned," Szoke said slowly, "is some information is best left buried. Especially when it wasn't ever supposed to happen."

"What wasn't supposed to happen?" she demanded.

Szoke glanced down at his watch.

"And what the hell are you waiting for?"

Szoke looked up, then seemed to catch sight of something over Carter's shoulder. Warily, she turned her head. A black limousine with tinted glass rolled toward them.

"Him," Szoke said simply.

"Who is this?" she asked.

Szoke didn't answer right away. He looked slightly sheepish. Then he said, "Sorry, Lori. He contacted me almost immediately when I started poking around about everything you told me."

"What's going on, Mark?"

This time, Szoke didn't reply at all. Instead, as soon as the vehicle stopped near them, Szoke walked toward it. Cautiously, Carter followed him. When they approached the rear window, the opaque glass slid downward. A well-groomed black man in his fifties sat in the seat. He looked out calmly at the two of them.

"Lori," Szoke said, waving his hand toward the man in the car. "This is Mr. Danforth." He turned toward Danforth. "And you already know Special Agent Lori Carter."

"I do." Danforth's voice was smooth and urbane. "Get in, Agent Carter. We have much to discuss."

13

Sandy wove through the crowd at the outdoor market, trying to blend into their numbers. He stopped at a coffee cart and stood in a short line, scanning the area with his peripheral vision.

No security.

No police.

Just people shopping for everything from food to clothes to electronics. It reminded Sandy of a cross between a farmer's market, a flea market, and a pod of food trucks all assembled together along the two blocks on the fringe of downtown. Although he'd seen several police vehicles pass by on the nearby street, none had stopped to investigate the shopping area.

Stay put for now, he thought. *Wait for darkness.*

Sandy ordered drip coffee and paid cash. He held the cup in both hands, sipping it as he walked through the area. He made sure to roughly match the pace and movement of the other shoppers.

At a homemade clothing stall, Sandy riffled through the selection of knit caps. He picked out a dark green one.

"How much?" he asked.

The woman behind the stall didn't glance up from her knitting. "Twenty," she said, her needles clacking rhythmically.

Sandy drew a twenty from his pocket and held it out to her. She lowered her knitting needles to accept it. Her eyes met Sandy's.

He saw no recognition there.

"Thank you," the woman said in a rote tone. She tucked the money into the metal cash box and resumed her work. He was all but forgotten. Just another customer.

That's good, Sandy thought, as he moved away. He pulled the cap onto his head. The fact that the woman didn't recognize him could mean the local police hadn't released his name and image to the public. This was a stroke of luck. Avoiding the police when they were actively searching for him was difficult enough. Managing to do so with an informed populace potentially watching for him as well was nigh on impossible.

Then again, he mused, perhaps the police had released his name and image, and like most people, the knitting woman simply didn't give a shit.

Sandy worked his way through the outdoor market, posing as a browser. When he reached the far edge, he considered taking another lap. The camouflage was good. He could get some food and kill some time until dark, when it would be easier to slip out of the area.

What he needed more than food, though, was some Tylenol. Something to fight the mounting fever and the congestion. But, for all its variety, the outdoor market didn't have a drug store.

The thought almost made Sandy grin. From what he could

tell, there *were* drugs changing hands. The dealers and users were subtle, but the exchanges were obvious to his practiced eye. Not that it did him any good. He was nowhere near desperate enough to need methamphetamine or some other illicit substance to keep him going. Some Sudafed would be enough.

That did make the corner of his mouth twitch in irony. Meth cooks commonly mined Sudafed for its pseudoephedrine. The legal cold drug was only a few chemical procedures away from its street cousin.

Sandy started to toss his empty coffee cup into the nearby trash can, then stopped. Even empty, he could hold it to his face and pretend to drink. It offered another element of disguise, so he kept it. He prepared to walk through the market again.

Then he saw a black and white pull to a stop at the far end. A pair of police officers exited. Sandy watched as they headed into the marketplace. He hoped they were only there for the food trucks. From experience, he knew cops were aware of all the best places to get a meal. If they were only looking for a rice bowl or a stuffed burrito, his hiding place would remain intact.

But the pair stood nearly shoulder-to-shoulder and adopted a pace Sandy immediately recognized. It would have been obvious to him even without the way each officer carefully scanned the ninety degrees on his side. They moved forward methodically, covering ground as swiftly as possible without rushing.

They were sweeping for him.

Sandy turned casually toward his right and stepped behind the nearest stall. His view of the officers was partially obstructed, but he knew he could see them far better than they could see him.

Hopefully, they were still looking for a man in a blue ball cap, not one in a dark green knit cap. He wished now he'd thought to buy a scarf from the knitting woman. Small accoutrements like that had an out-sized impact on how much they changed a person's appearance.

The pair of officers continued to move forward, slicing through the crowd with easy confidence and clear concentration.

Sandy strode away to his own right. When he reached the sidewalk, he shuffled to the corner and punched the crosswalk button. Behind him, he imagined one of the officers spotting him. Calling out to his partner and pointing. The pair breaking into a run. Could he outrun them, fever and all?

Probably.

He was less likely to outrun a radio.

From the looks of it, there were plenty of police cars in the area.

Sandy resisted the urge to glance over his shoulder. He stood still and waited. After what seemed like an hour, the light changed and a white walk signal appeared. Along with several other people, Sandy made his way across the street. He turned to his left as soon as he reached the opposite sidewalk. Out of the corner of his eye, he looked for his pursuers.

Nothing.

The searching officers were hidden somewhere behind the rows of stalls.

He'd escaped.

Sandy put his hands in his coat pockets and trudged forward. He had to find a new hiding place.

He'd gone hardly a block when another patrol car passed by, this one with a single officer behind the wheel. Sandy avoided looking that direction, not wanting to invite eye contact from the driver.

Once the car was out of sight, Sandy cut into an alley. It was long, running for what appeared to be a double block. A dozen dumpsters lined the walls.

It was perfect.

Find a resting spot behind one of the dumpsters and wait for dark, he told himself. Then slip out of downtown to more of a suburb and steal another car. Milwaukee was still a good option as a place to lay over until he felt better. His cash would last that long, at least.

Sandy hurried down the alley. The first two dumpsters he checked sat flush against the wall. The third was at a slight angle near a small loading ramp, creating a garbage-strewn nook behind it. Sandy started to duck into the area when suddenly the garbage moved.

The dirty, bearded man in tattered clothing rolled up onto his haunches. Growling, he extended a knife toward Sandy.

"Find your own goddamned home!"

Sandy held his hands up and backed away. Once he was clear of the opening, he hustled further down the alley. Four dumpsters later, he found a different one with space behind it. This one was unoccupied. Sandy dug a battered cardboard box from the dumpster and quickly flattened it. Then, crouching, he duck-walked behind the metal container until he reached the deepest corner. He laid the cardboard on the asphalt and settled down on top of it.

His back to the wall, Sandy kept his ears pricked for movement close by. He stared at the small opening that led to his temporary sanctuary. The weight of his .45 under his jacket was reassuring, but firing a gun wasn't something he wanted to be forced to do. Right now, stealth was his best option. Going loud was the option of last resort.

Sandy drew his coat close around himself and rested his head back against the brick wall. A wave of exhaustion hit him, making his lids heavy. He forced himself to stare at the one point of ingress to his hiding place.

Wait until dark, he reminded himself.

After the months of comparative safety at Hank's ranch,

being actively pursued again was a jolt to Sandy. He'd experienced a general sense of unease at the ranch, but it was nothing like this. They'd been searching for him before.

Now, he was being hunted.

He felt like he was behind enemy lines once again.

Sandy sat and stared at the opening. He listened to the mundane city sounds while his cheeks burned with fever. He fought sleep as his eyes continued to droop. His thoughts leapt from Cal to Brophy to Janet. He tried to focus on that last image, but couldn't. Instead, it was another face that followed him down when he finally surrendered to sleep.

14

1982

He waited in front of the cabin.

"Three days," his cousin Mayford told the boy before he departed in his truck. "If I'm not back by then, something went wrong. That happens, you need to light out on your own."

The sun was now waning on that third day. Shafts of sunlight pierced through the trees, creating a mottled light pattern on the forest floor. He sat in Mayford's chair on the porch and watched for any sign of his older cousin. The idea the man might not return wasn't something he wanted to consider.

Light out on my own? He wondered. He knew he'd have to do so, but a larger question loomed.

And go where?

The pain of his mother's death still burned in his gut. He'd barely been able to contain his rage when the police came to the house. Especially when they treated it all like it was a natural event. Even the medics had called it heart failure. The coroner's brief investigation agreed—she died of heart failure brought on by alcoholism.

He knew better.

Errol was responsible. All the beatings, all the constant abuse, demeaning her, frightening her. All the guilt she felt for choosing to be with him. For not being able to leave him. For what he did to her son.

He saw it all. That was how he knew. Her heart may have failed, but it wasn't the booze. It was already broken into a hundred jagged pieces, and Errol was the one who broke it.

He ground his teeth and stared deep into the woods, watching for Cousin Mayford.

The funeral was the hardest part. All the pious sympathy from people who knew damn well how Errol treated her. He couldn't endure the charade to the end and left early.

That night, Errol drank more heavily than normal. As usual, the man went from morose to angry in a short time. He went looking for his customary target to take out his anger, but she wasn't there anymore. So, he turned to his second choice.

"I'll show you what a big man can do," he threatened, repeating his oft-uttered phrase as he loomed above the young man.

This time was different, though.

The extra booze made him slower and less coordinated. As the two came to blows, it wasn't the forty-five-year-old roofer that delivered the damage. It was the bereaved son, all of eighteen years, who pushed back. It was over in a few scant seconds. His fishing knife slid from his belt. One quick slashing motion opened Errol's throat. The drunken man staggered back in surprise and collapsed onto the couch, clutching at his throat with both hands.

He watched Errol as confusion filled his eyes, then gave way to hate before they emptied of any emotion entirely. Errol's desperate fingers slid away from the gaping wound below his chin. They landed heavily in his lap with a wet slap.

I should have done this years ago. Maybe she would still be alive.

He watched a while longer, to be sure.

Then he ran.

He spent the night crashing through the forest, looking for Mayford's cabin. It was well after dawn when his cousin found him, dirty, exhausted, huddled by a tree, with Errol's blood still caked on his hands and shirt.

To his credit, Mayford never asked him a single question. He brought him to his cabin, fed him, and let him rest. Later, they spoke only briefly.

"Son of a bitch got what he had coming," Mayford told him. "If he'd ever stepped foot outside of town again, I'd have done for him myself." He patted the young man on the shoulder. "You done right by your mother, boy. Roy would've been proud of you."

Mayford's words made the boy tear up. He struggled not to burst out crying while Mayford squeezed his shoulder. His own memories of his father were those of a young boy, but Mayford had known Roy as a man. First cousins here in Tennessee were as tight as brothers, so he knew Mayford spoke with some authority.

They settled into a quiet routine for several weeks. No one came to the cabin. He wasn't sure if anyone even knew exactly where to find it. Mayford went into town, ostensibly for supplies, and returned with news. The sheriff was publicly calling it a horrible murder, but the whispers Mayford heard around town were most thought Errol got what he had coming.

"Maybe I should turn myself in, then," he'd suggested. The idea that a sympathetic jury might let him off sprang into his head like a beacon of hope.

"Don't be stupid," Mayford said, crushing the thought before it fully formed. His cousin was a few years older than his father would have been and the lines of his craggy face showed it. His eyes burned fiercely when he spoke. "What people whisper doesn't change what they'll do. You get caught, they'll try you for murder, sure as I'm sitting here. No chance in hell you're not found guilty, and that's the needle, son."

"Well, I can't stay here. They'll find me eventually and then you'll go to prison, too."

"Don't you worry none about me."

"You're family," he said. Then he realized something else. "You're all the family I have left. I can't stay."

Mayford had looked at him long and hard after he spoke, squinting in thought. Finally, he said, "All right. I know if I say otherwise, you'll just sneak off some night anyway. Probably get caught in the process."

He didn't reply, but his cousin was right about that.

"Stay here a spell longer while I try something," Mayford told him. "I might know someone who can help."

In the morning, Mayford departed, giving him the three-day warning as he left.

And so, he sat and waited, while the sun dipped lower in the sky, and finally disappeared. No one arrived. Disappointed, he went inside and made himself something to eat. Then he gathered his things together. He'd leave at first light. If he could, he'd find a way to say goodbye to Janet. Then… what? A life of hiding, on the run?

He swallowed hard and stared into the fire. There, he found the truth. It was either hide or go to prison.

He poked at the fire, causing a cluster of sparks to flare up. Then he waited.

It was well after dark, when the cabin door rattled and

Cousin Mayford returned. He noticed the young man's startled expression, as well as the pack leaning against the small bunk. He smiled and nodded. "Glad you listened," he said. "That's a tendency that'll help where you're going."

He sat on the edge of the bed, rubbing his eyes. "Where's that?"

Mayford shrugged off his own pack and stood in front of the dwindling fire, rubbing his hands. "Check my pack," he said. "Outside pocket."

He stared at his cousin for a moment, wondering what the man was up to. Then he rose and obeyed. In the outside pocket, he drew out an envelope.

"Open it," said Mayford.

He pushed aside the flap. Inside was a single piece of paper folded into thirds. When he pulled it from the envelope, a small card slid out the end and dropped to the floor at his feet.

"Don't lose that," Mayford chided him. "You're gonna need it."

He unfolded the paper and examined it. Then he looked over at Mayford. "A birth certificate?"

His cousin nodded. "Keegan Anthony Fuller," he said. "Born same year as you. His social security number's written on the back." He pointed down to the young man's feet. "And that's a school ID with his name on it."

He picked it up. His own photo stared up at him. He recognized it as his school picture from just a few months ago. "So, I… I say I'm him?"

"That's the idea."

"What if he—"

"There are no what ifs where he's concerned. Keegan isn't going to be using his name, son. He died when he was three."

He digested the news, then lifted the fake school ID. "What am I supposed to use this for?"

"Sorry I couldn't swing a driver's license, but this'll do."

"Do for what?"

Mayford grinned at him. "Go to Memphis and join the army. They're in a big push right now. This paperwork is all the ID you'll need."

"The army?" The thought had never occurred to him.

Mayford nodded. "Go infantry. They won't look too hard into where you come from if you're a ground pounder. As soon as they issue you that military identification, you'll *be* Keegan Fuller."

He shook his head, partially in amazement, partially in disbelief. "Will this work?"

"Of course, it will."

"What if it doesn't, though?" He looked up from the documents to meet Mayford's gaze. "What if they find out who I really am?"

Mayford gave him a hard stare. "It's a better choice than running. You do a good job and, even if somewhere down the line they figure it all out, you'll be a hero. No one hangs a hero."

15

"You're on dangerous ground, here, Agent Carter."

Danforth spoke easily while they rode in the limo, but she could hear the menace beneath his polished tone.

"How is working my case—"

Danforth held up a hand to stop her. Carter noticed his short nails were perfectly manicured. "Let's not play pretend. That's for the world out there." He pointed out the window. "In here, we deal with real truths."

"All right," she said carefully. "And what's the real truth here?"

"The truth is you're not just chasing a fugitive. You are digging into events that don't concern you. Events you don't need to know in order to catch this man."

"I don't agree."

"Your agreement is moot. What I am telling you is all that matters."

She stared at him. The dissonance between the words he spoke and his visage as an elegant businessman with a smooth voice clanged in her ears. "Are you telling me to back off?"

"On searching for Sandy Banks? No. But as for trying to unravel the man's past? Yes."

"His past is the key to finding him."

"Perhaps. But it isn't something you need to be delving into, Agent Carter."

"I'm not going to quit."

Danforth's eyebrow arched slightly. "Even at the cost of your career?"

Carter scowled. "Don't threaten me."

"It's not a threat. It's a question."

She glanced over at Szoke, who sat silently beside Danforth. "If you know anything about me," she said to Danforth, "you know I'm willing to take that risk."

"Risking a career is one thing," he replied. "What about your life?"

Her eyes narrowed. Danforth's expression remained placid. She kept her gaze on his face, but noted both men's hands were visible and empty. If she had to, could she draw before either of them got to their weapons? She didn't know for certain if either one was even armed, but she had to assume so.

"Are we actually going to the airport?" she asked. "Or are you taking me to some black site?"

"The airport, I assure you. Now, answer the question."

"I've put my life on the line plenty of times," Carter said.

"Yes, for justice," Danforth replied. "But for knowledge?"

She was quiet for a few seconds. Then she said in a low tone, "Sometimes knowing *is* justice."

Danforth considered, then shrugged. "I wonder if you might be one of the last true believers, Agent Carter." She opened her mouth to reply but he waved away her response. "It doesn't matter. We all have our tragic flaws, don't we? I'll concede this much—it is clear you won't let this go. And it would be a terrible waste of talent to bounce you from the Bureau. Thus, we shall have to use those talents."

He leaned forward slightly.

"First," he said, "I need to tell you a story."

16

1985
Honduras

"**Y**ou come back to me, William Sutter."

Janet's words rang in his ears every night as he fell asleep. They floated in the air while he went first through basic training, then advanced infantry training. They faded but never left him when he was selected for this unit and underwent the harsh training to finally qualify. Along the way, he truly became Keegan Fuller. Once they put the patch on his uniform and he and his classmates raised their beer bottles in celebrations, he had enough time to catch his breath, and the words returned to haunt him.

So did his reply.

"I will. I promise."

And he would, he knew. He didn't know how, or when, but

he would keep his promise. He would stay alive and somehow return to her. He couldn't do it as William Sutter—that person had disappeared from this world—but Keegan Fuller could do it.

Just not yet.

The lieutenant motioned toward the map while he spoke. Keegan watched and listened carefully, pushing Janet's words down deep inside.

"The suits are calling this Project Seedkiller," said Lieutenant Culliver. To Keegan, he had the look of a prep school graduate. Someone who played lacrosse and was allowed to drink martinis at dinner with his parents at sixteen. "This is a direct action."

Keegan didn't react, but he felt both Brophy and Lloyd glance toward him.

"The target is Miguel Chavarria. He's the nephew of a Ramon Chavarria, a Sandinista on the rise. Intelligence believes Miguel will rise right along with his uncle. Ramon is already too high profile of a target, but the suits believe a preemptive strike on Miguel is still low visibility."

Keegan knew what that meant. The CIA believed they could get away with this assassination without causing an uproar. If they projected Miguel to be a bigwig later on down the line, he'd eventually be too high profile for direct action.

"Chavarria has command of a small unit near the Honduran border." Lieutenant Culliver punched at the map on the display board with his index finger. "It is essentially a border patrol posting, designed to give him some command time and build his credibility, to prop up his resume. But apparently Miguel is a bit of a showboat. Instead of staying at the command post, he likes to get out in the field and strut around. That presents this opportunity. Questions so far?"

Keegan gave the platoon leader one short shake of his head.

"Good. Now, standard directives apply here. FDN operatives will be primary on this op. This is their war, after all. You will accompany them in an advisory role. When they make their incursion into Nicaragua, you stay on Honduran soil. Clear?"

"Roger that," said Keegan.

"You three are our eyes and ears on this one. Not that we don't trust our freedom-fighting brothers in arms or anything but we'd still like independent verification on the target. That's your mission. The rest of the platoon will remain here, providing intelligence support and exfil, if you need it." Culliver looked at each man in turn. "Any other questions?"

"No, sir," the three responded in unison.

"Then get your gear ready, and good luck."

Keegan cringed at the final words. Nothing ensured a bad mission more than wishing a soldier good luck.

True to form, their luck was bad from the jump. One of the FDN Contras broke—or at least badly sprained—his ankle in a ravine thirty minutes outside of base camp, so two other squad members had to escort him back. Aguilar, the squad leader, directed them to drop him off at the medic station, secure a replacement squad member, and return quickly. Then, as the trio hustled back through the bush the way they'd come, Aguilar opted to press on without them. This was despite Keegan's advice to stay put.

"Gear up," Keegan ordered, once Aguilar disregarded his counsel.

"Bad idea, Sarge," Brophy muttered.

Keegan shrugged. "His op. We're just here to advise. I can't make him listen."

Nearby Lloyd performed a radio check, then sent a coded message back to Culliver to advise him of the development.

Keegan noticed Aguilar's radio operator didn't do likewise.

"*Vamos,*" Aguilar urged them, waving his arm forward.

"Yeah, yeah," Brophy said. "We're goddamn vamosing."

The group reached the border a little over an hour later. Keegan and his men took up positions in the tree line above the roadway that marked the border. Aguilar crossed into Nicaraguan territory with his squad and set up on the opposite side of the road, where he waited impatiently for the rest of his squad. An hour passed, then two. Keegan alternated between scanning the surrounding countryside with his field glasses and using them to check up on Aguilar. By the end of the third hour, Aguilar's irritation had grown to barely suppressed rage. He seemed to utter a curse and waved to his radio operator, obviously issuing an order. Keegan had no doubt it was to contact the command post and check on the status of his remaining squad members.

Before the radioman could comply, a slow moving patrol vehicle appeared half a kilometer down the road.

"Heads up!" Keegan told Brophy and Lloyd.

Brophy adjusted his sniper rifle, training it on the jeep-like vehicle as it crawled forward. "Got it."

Aguilar spotted the patrol as well. He and his squad dropped into hiding and waited. At almost half-strength, Keegan couldn't imagine the FDN sergeant would launch an attack on the patrol. Then again, if Chavarria was present...

Keegan trained his field glasses onto the approaching vehicle. He counted a driver, an officer in the passenger seat and three men in the rear. One of the soldiers cradled a light machine gun across his thighs while the other two were equipped with rifles.

"I've got two AKs in the rear," Keegan said, "and an RPD."

"Confirmed," said Brophy. He adjusted his position slightly. "The officer is a captain. Not Chavarria. Repeat, *not* the target."

"Got it," Keegan said.

Aguilar had to be seeing the same thing, he knew. That meant they'd let this patrol pass. According to their intel, another one would be along within three hours. Perhaps Chavarria would be out playing soldier on that one. If not, the fallback plan was to wait for dark and Aguilar's team would go further in-country and try to snipe the target at the border patrol command post. It was a much riskier approach, and Keegan hoped the op didn't break that way.

Still, this patrol being a miss wasn't all bad. It would allow for the rest of Aguilar's team to arrive and…

"They're slowing down," Brophy said, his voice barely audible.

Keegan noticed it, too. He pressed the glasses to his face and trained them on the Sandinista officer in the passenger seat. He was around forty, trim, with a hawk-like face. His expression was hard and wary as he lowered the radio microphone. His gaze was fixed on the area where Aguilar's squad was hidden.

How can they see anything? I can't.

"They're burned," Brophy said, his tone certain.

Keegan watched for several long moments. Then the captain seemed satisfied he hadn't actually seen anything of note and ordered the driver to continue. The jeep surged forward, resuming its patrol. Keegan followed them as they rolled along the rugged jungle road.

Suddenly, the vehicle whipped to the left, angling toward Aguilar's position. The soldiers leaped from the back, training their rifles on the Contras's hidden location. The machine gunner dropped to his belly and expertly set up his weapon. The driver flopped down next to him, obviously pulling double duty as the a-gunner and ammunition feeder.

The captain called out in Spanish. Keegan's rudimentary command of the language plus the distance made it hard to make out the exact words. But the message was clear—*surrender.*

Aguilar didn't respond. No one in the squad moved.

The captain shouted his orders again, this time more forcefully.

No response.

That's what I would do, Keegan thought. *Wait him out. See if he decides he's seeing ghosts and leaves.*

Then Aguilar opened fire.

The M-16s crackled and spit through the jungle, tearing into the patrol vehicle. The captain crouched behind the comparative safety of the front wheel while his own troops returned fire. The AK-47s and the RPD poured lead toward Aguilar's position. Keegan watched as leaves, branches, and bark leapt and spun in the air, torn by a hail of bullets.

"Sarge?" Brophy asked him.

"Hold fire," Keegan answered automatically, even though the order galled him. The rules of engagement were clear. They were not to leave Honduran soil nor fire upon any foreign combatants unless fired upon themselves.

The trio watched the exchange of gunfire for a few more seconds.

"At least it's a fair fight," Keegan muttered, his words mostly torn apart by the loud cracks of the rifles.

He'd spoken too soon, however. A second patrol vehicle roared down the roadway, approaching from the same direction as the first. Six more soldiers were crammed into the back, including another machine-gunner. The driver slid to a halt, positioning them so that Aguilar's depleted squad was now triangulated.

"They're going to get torn apart," Brophy warned.

Keegan knew he was right.

Before the second squad could open fire, a third vehicle, this one a transport truck rumbled around the bend and rolled toward the firefight. He recognized the Soviet model immediately and knew it could easily hold up to sixteen soldiers.

Keegan cursed. Options flashed through his mind. Lieutenant Culliver's rules of engagement were clear—they were not to fire unless fired upon, and then only to defend themselves as they retreated. But if he didn't act now, Aguilar's entire squad would be chewed to bits.

He raised his M-16.

"Take out the gunners first," he told Brophy.

Then he chose a target and fired.

17

"You're disgusted," Danforth said to Carter. "I can tell."

From her seat across from him in the back of the limousine, Carter crossed her arms and lifted her shoulders in a bare shrug. "I'm well past being surprised at hearing some of the dark shit you people have done over the years."

Danforth raised a brow. "You people?" he repeated.

She smirked. "Don't try that. You know what I mean."

"I know what you *said*, Agent Carter."

"Point is," she continued, "what I'm hearing *you* say is we pulled the same shit in Nicaragua in '83 that we did in Vietnam two decades earlier. I didn't *know* it—I doubt many people did, in fact—but I'm not surprised by it. You people are always meddling."

"*We people*," Danforth said, sarcasm seeping into his words, "are always trying to keep our nation safe. Sometimes that requires coloring outside the lines."

"Then why have lines in the first place?"

"Is that a real question?" His expression shifted to one of light amusement. "You don't know the answer already?"

"Pretend I don't. Indulge me."

"It's simple enough. The lines are an important fiction. They keep most of the world in check."

Carter frowned. "That's about what I expected you to say."

"You have a different view?"

"I have the correct view."

Danforth waved for her to continue.

"It's nothing earth-shattering," said Carter. "Laws are in place to protect the well-being of the people."

Danforth shook his head. "I wonder if you'll be able to shed that illusion, Agent Carter."

"It's not an illusion."

"So, you're saying that is how the world works, then? We pass a law and everyone magically follows it?"

"No. It's an ideal we strive for."

"Ah. And along the way, the people responsible for dealing with those who won't obey the law are constrained by that very law themselves… and often unable to hold those lawbreakers accountable because of that adherence."

"You're starting to sound sympathetic to the vigilante group Banks was part of in Spokane. Was that your operation?"

"No," Danforth admitted. "but you have to admire the karmic simplicity of it, don't you?"

"It was murder," Carter said. "Just like what you've described him doing in Nicaragua was an illegal, secret war."

Danforth tilted his head slightly. "I am worried for you."

Carter glanced over at Szoke and then around the limousine interior. "What, are we not going to the airport, after all?"

"I don't mean your personal safety. You are in no danger and our destination *is* the airfield. No, I mean your mental well-being."

Carter scoffed. "I'll be fine."

"Famous last words." Danforth smiled tightly. "I think you are an idealist at heart, Agent Carter. True, the grinding years in this career have nearly transformed you into a realist. But you stubbornly hang on to the last vestiges of that idealism, don't you? That is a dangerous combination. For any person, really, but especially for someone in law enforcement."

Irritation flickered in her. Who was this guy, thinking he *knew* her?

"Why's that?" she demanded.

"Because we all know the idealist in you will eventually be crushed. Not only that but, thanks to the growing realist in you, you will see that train coming down the tracks. Perhaps, you already do."

Carter leaned forward and jabbed a finger toward him. "Look, pal, don't act like you know me."

"I'm not acting."

"And don't lecture me, either."

"I wouldn't presume. You did ask the question. In any event, I'm merely stating facts. And telling you a story."

"Not a very useful one. I still haven't heard anything that will help me find Sandy Banks today."

"Very well. I'll finish the story, then. If you want me to, that is."

"Can we just stop with this…" She waved her hand briefly, struggling to find the right word. "This performance?" she finished. "If you have a point, get to it."

"The point of this story is in the telling," said Danforth. "But let's get to the end and see if it meets with your approval. And your expectations."

"I expect things to end badly," she said.

"Doesn't every story end that way?" Danforth asked. "Eventually?"

18

1985
Nicaragua

The bark and spit of gunfire surrounded them. Even though their initial shots took the Sandinista squads by surprise and disrupted their flanking maneuver, the soldiers recovered. Now, rounds whistled through the trees and bushes, ripping through foliage like homicidal bees.

When Keegan heard movement, behind their position, his first thought was the remnants of Aguilar's squad had finally caught up to them. He turned to order them to fan out on the right flank.

And froze.

Six Nicaraguan regulars leveled their rifles at them.

Shit.

They were dead.

One of the soldiers fired a round that struck the ground near Brophy. The sniper looked over his shoulder. Keegan tensed to whip his M-16 around to take at least one of the enemy with him.

Then he saw the NCO raise his hand and give the cease-fire signal while he repeated the order aloud. Next to him, a radio operator relayed the message. A few moments later, the sound of gunfire fell off and then stopped entirely.

"Americanos," the NCO said, his face betraying his disgust. Then he spoke in heavily accented English. "Hands up. All."

Keegan uncurled his grip from his rifle. Slowly, he raised his hands in surrender. To his left and right, Brophy and Lloyd did the same.

"Knees!" ordered the NCO.

The three men faced the Sandinista soldiers and rose up from their bellies to their knees, almost as one.

Keegan waited for them to shoot. He didn't welcome death, but he thought this would at least be a good one. His only regret in that moment was he would never keep his promise to Janet.

But the Nicaraguans had other plans.

The makeshift cage was too small for them to stand. Shoeless and stripped down to their undergarments, Keegan and Brophy squatted inside the twisted metal that reminded him of chicken wire.

"He's been gone longer than you were," Keegan observed.

"I know."

Both kept their voices barely above a whisper. The Sandinista guard that stood nearby had screamed *"Silencio!"* at them every time they'd spoken earlier, so much of their early conversation had been via hand signals. That method was limited, however. When a shift-change occurred, the replacement guard stood further away and appeared less interested in either of them. They managed to communicate now in hushed tones.

"How hard did they go at you?" Keegan asked.

Brophy shook his head. "Not hard at all. Some captain did most of the talking. His English was good."

Keegan frowned. "Figures. We probably trained him."

Brophy turned his head and spat. "It's not the captain I'm worried about. It's the sergeant in there that will be a problem. Smaller guy, but intense. He got really agitated when he tried to pull my dog tags."

"Wait, what?"

"He tried to yank my tags. Joke was on him, though."

"You didn't wear your tags?" Keegan asked.

Brophy shook his head. "I figured this was considered a covert op, so I dumped them in my tent before we left. I thought everyone did."

Keegan didn't reply. Everyone should have, he realized. As squad leader, that mistake was on him.

"They're going to do me ugly because of it," Brophy said. "They'll think I'm fucking CIA."

"They'll interrogate me first," Keegan told him. "They'll assume you'll be the most difficult nut to crack, so they'll try to get a better baseline of information before they start on round two with you." He turned his gaze toward the interview tent, forty meters away. "Might be they're already getting some of that."

"Evan's solid."

"We're all solid," Keegan said. "But everyone breaks at some point."

Brophy uttered a curse. "No one is coming for us, are they?"

Keegan shook his head.

Brophy spat. "So much for never leaving a brother behind."

"I guess it doesn't count, since we're not really here at all."

"What's the plan?"

Keegan glanced up at the sun as it dipped low. "Wait for dark. Make a break when one of us is either coming or going from the interrogation tent."

"They'll be expecting that."

Keegan thought about it. "Maybe." He shrugged. "Probably. But maybe they'll also be so over the moon they captured three Americans that their guard will come down."

"Or we'll get the maximum security treatment."

"If we ever leave this camp, that's coming," Keegan agreed. "But until then, we've got a shot."

"Until dark, then?"

"Until dark," Keegan said.

Lloyd returned to the cage as dusk threatened. His face bore a few marks but he wasn't badly beaten. The haunted look in his eyes worried Keegan more.

"They know everything," he reported.

"What did you tell them?"

"Nothing. They already knew."

"Did you confirm anything?"

Lloyd shook his head dully. "Only what's on my tags. The officer in charge, the captain, he's very pleased with himself." He paused. "Chavarria was there, too."

Keegan's eyes widened at that. "Our intel was good, then," he murmured. Then he dismissed the information. "The mission is scrubbed. Our mission now is one hundred percent SERE."

He looked back and forth between the two soldiers to en-sure they understood.

Survival.

Evasion.

Resistance.

Escape.

Brophy and Lloyd met his gaze with steel, resolute expres-sions.

"Good," Keegan said. "We go the next time that cage door opens. Clear?"

Both men nodded.

The three of them settled in to wait for darkness.

They didn't make it.

Just a few minutes later, three soldiers approached the cage. Two carried rifles and flanked a compact man wearing the insignia of a sergeant. He paused near the door and pointed at Keegan. He spoke in Spanish too rapidly for Kee-gan to pick out the words with his limited comprehension of the language, but it didn't matter. The message was clear.

It was his turn.

One of the soldiers leveled his rifle at Brophy and Lloyd. He jerked the barrel, ordering them to the far side of the cage.

Reluctantly, the two men crab-walked in that direction.

Keegan quickly assessed the situation. Then he said, "It's not as dark as it looks." He kept his voice low, intending that only his comrades heard him, and that they understood his message. If their captors caught his words, he hoped their vague nature would escape notice.

The second soldier shouldered his rifle and unlocked the cage. Then he stepped back and waved his hand at Keegan.

"Venga!" he ordered.

Keegan crawled slowly out the door. He exaggerated his

soreness to disguise his own agility. The soldier barked his order again, but Keegan didn't react. When he stood, the man quickly bound his wrists in front with a short section of rope. Then the soldier unshouldered his rifle and reached out with his left arm to push him forward.

Despite his coded message to Brophy and Lloyd to stand down, Keegan almost reversed his decision in that moment. But he resisted the urge. There were three of them. His hands were tied. The odds were too great. He would wait for a better chance.

If you get one.

He knew he would, though. The chances of success would be higher when they returned him to the cage. It would be dark, if nothing else.

That was *if* he returned, of course.

He absorbed the hard shove and stumbled forward several steps. Behind him, he heard the soldier lock the cage door. A moment later, he was shoved again. He staggered for a step, then dropped into a slow, shuffling gait. The sergeant walked ahead of him, setting the pace. When Keegan didn't match it, the escorting soldiers shoved him forward.

When they reached a large tent, he was hustled inside. A captain in a pressed uniform stood beside a military field desk. Keegan took in the familiar style before realizing it was the same exact model as the one in Lieutenant Carrick's headquarters tent. He was almost certainly looking at a re-purposed relic from the Somoza regime. A thought shot through his mind, something about Romans being killed with their own swords. Before it could sufficiently form, he was thrust into a low chair in the middle of the room.

No Chavarria, he thought. *Maybe he'll join us later.*

The captain eyed him imperiously. Keegan reflected back nothing; no defiance, no fear. He made himself a blank slate.

The captain frowned slightly. He jerked his head. The sergeant stepped forward, reached out and grasped the chain around his neck. He tugged sharply, and the chain snapped. The sergeant turned and handed the dog tags to the captain. The officer took them without looking at them. His eyes remained fixed on Keegan.

Finally, he spoke in barely accented English. "I am *Capitan* Jaquin. This is *Sergeante* Rivas. And you are clearly American, are you not?"

"Keegan Fuller," he replied. "Sergeant."

The captain tilted his head.

Keegan began to recite his serial number, which was his social security number. The sergeant stepped forward and struck him across the face with an open hand. Keegan braced for the slap but the force of the blow stunned him and knocked him from the chair.

This Sergeant Rivas knows how to hit.

Keegan's ears rang momentarily. The left side of his face burned hotly. After a moment, he struggled to his feet. The sergeant shoved him back into the chair.

Captain Jaquin held up his dog tags. "I have no need of your recitation, Sergeant. That information is already mine. There is other information I require, however."

Keegan didn't reply.

"What is your mission?" Jaquin asked.

Keegan waited a beat. Then he said, "Keegan Fuller. Sergeant. Five, three, two—"

Sergeant Rivas's left hand flashed and struck him, this time on the opposite side of the face. Keegan toppled from the chair once more, stunned. On all fours, he stared at the tent floor, shaking his head to clear his senses. When he didn't rise on his own, Rivas grabbed him by the shoulders. His vise-like grip forced him to his feet and back into the chair.

Captain Jaquin made a chiding sound. "Sergeant Fuller,

this is not how I want our conversation to go. Rest assured, we are going to speak about your mission in my country with great particularity. This is not in question. The only question is how long before we have the salient part of the conversation?"

Keegan touched his tongue to a jagged tear on the inside of his mouth, tasting blood.

"If you choose, there lies a very hard road between this moment and that. But why travel on it at all? Your companion did not."

An image of Lloyd sprang into Keegan's mind. He forced himself to recall the soldier's words. Lloyd had said he didn't talk. Keegan knew he needed to keep reminding himself of that.

No one talked.

Jaquin is bluffing.

The captain's smile was insincere. "Yes, I already know everything, Sergeant. Who you are, what your mission was, all of it. Or, at least, I know what young Evan told me. I think it is likely he lied about some of it. That is where you come in. I expect you to help me to… how do you say it in America? Separate the wheat from the chaff?"

Keegan glanced around the tent. The two escorts had withdrawn to just outside the doorway. Aside from Captain Jaquin, Sergeant Rivas was the only other man present. Keegan wondered where Chavarria had gone.

"Shall we begin our collaboration?" Jaquin asked.

Keegan met his gaze. "Where'd you learn English?"

"It doesn't matter."

"Was it SOA?" Keegan asked. He watched the captain's eyes for any hint of recognition at the abbreviation for the School of the Americas. When he saw a flicker there, he forged ahead. "If we trained you, that means you were part of Somoza's regime. Now, you're an officer in the regime that overthrew him. So, that begs a question, doesn't it?"

Jaquin signaled Rivas, who struck him once more. This blow came straight at him, catching the tip of his nose and powering through. Keegan's head snapped backward. His body followed and the chair tipped. He crashed to the ground. His shoulders hit first, then his head.

Keegan groaned and didn't move.

Rivas didn't give him any respite. The sergeant pulled Keegan and the chair upright. Keegan stared at Captain Jaquin, his eyes watering.

"You were saying?" Jaquin said smoothly.

Keegan turned his head and spat a bloody glob onto the tent floor. "I was saying either you were a traitor then or you're a traitor now."

Rivas stepped forward. The Nicaraguan sergeant obviously comprehended more English than either man let on. Jaquin held up his hand to stop him. "What do you know of my country? Little or less, I imagine. Do not think you have any idea what constitutes a traitor or a patriot. Instead, you should be more concerned about what constitutes a spy."

"I'm not a spy," Keegan said. "I know what I am. Do you? When the Contras take over, are you just going to flit on over to that side, like a—"

Jaquin dropped his hand.

Rivas hit him again.

And so it went, for another hour. Keegan did his best to tell Jaquin nothing. He knew he should have refused to say a single word outside of his name, rank, and serial number. Whenever he tried to revert to that formula, Jaquin reminded him the Geneva convention did not apply.

"Our nations are not at war," the velvet-toned captain said. "Not a declared one, anyway. That is what makes your presence here either espionage or a declaration of war. Which one is for the generals and politicians to decide."

After that, Keegan kept his replies to a minimum. He said just enough to prolong the interrogation, to ensure full darkness had fallen before he was returned to the cage.

From outside the tent, sounds of festivity reached his ears.

Jaquin saw him notice and smiled. "My men are jubilant," he explained. "We have captured the mighty Americans. We now have proof of your country's naked support for the rebels. They are not the ignorant third world men you no doubt think they are. They understand the implications. Exposing your presence here will be a black eye for the US. Your President Reagan's own Francis Gary Powers, as it were. He will be forced to discontinue support for the Contras. After that, it is only a matter of time until this war is over."

Keegan didn't respond, but he heard the truth in Jaquin's words. He envisioned himself and his team paraded before the press for propaganda purposes. He knew it would play out exactly as the captain described.

He shook off the thought. Like Jaquin pointed out, those were concerns for generals and politicians. He was a soldier with a mission.

Despite the grim outlook, he never stopped trying to glean intelligence from the situation. He made note of every question Jaquin asked and tried to commit them to memory. When they escaped, he would repeat the information to intelligence officers during the debrief.

Escape.

Survive.

He forced himself to believe in both.

Finally, Jaquin lifted his hands in mock frustration. "I have engaged with you in good faith, Sergeant. We both know the inevitability of the situation. You *will* eventually talk. I recognize your duty as a soldier to resist, but hasn't that duty been fulfilled? Does it require you to be beaten within an inch of your life?"

Keegan didn't reply to that.

Jaquin sighed. "Very well. I shall turn this matter over to Sergeant Rivas. His patience is significantly less than mine. And his tactics are… more direct."

Next to Jaquin, Rivas stared flatly at Keegan. The lack of emotion on the sergeant's face was more menacing than if he'd adopted a snarling visage.

"Are you hungry?" Jaquin asked. "I imagine you are. I know I am. So, I'm going to enjoy a nice meal with Sergeant Rivas. Then he will proceed to work on extracting the information I need from you. If, during our dinner, you and your companions re-think your position, I would advise you to make that clear early on in the questioning process."

Once more, Keegan didn't answer.

Jaquin called for the guards, who lifted Keegan by the arms and escorted him from the tent. Rivas did not join them. Keegan moved along with a labored gait, exaggerating his own injury. This time, the soldiers did little to prod him forward.

As they neared the cage, Keegan made eye contact with Brophy. He gave the corporal a barely perceptible nod. To be certain his message was delivered, he blinked rapidly. Brophy gave no outward sign he understood, but Keegan noticed the slight shift in his crouching stance. The corporal looked to be subtly loading his weight backward as if preparing to spring forward.

He knows.

Keegan waited until the first soldier shouldered his weapon and undid the latch. He swung open the cage door and waved for Keegan to enter. Instead, Keegan held out his bound hands to be untied.

The soldier jerked his head angrily. He motioned toward the cage again.

Keegan extended his hands further, as if he didn't understand.

"No," the soldier said. He glanced at the soldier behind Keegan and said something in rapid Spanish.

The second soldier shoved Keegan. Keegan let his knees buckle and collapsed to the ground.

The first soldier frowned and stepped toward him. In the same moment, Keegan felt the muzzle of the rifle press to the base of his neck.

Now is the time.

Keegan leaned hard to the side and whirled to his feet. Stepping forward, he whipped his bound hands like a baseball swing. Keegan looked into the man's surprised eyes as the bottom of both fists crashed into the man's jaw. Then the eyes went unfocused. The soldier's knees buckled but, unlike when he'd done it moments ago, this was no feint.

Without hesitation, Keegan stepped behind the man and threaded his arm over the top of his head. He clamped his neck between his own forearms and squeezed. He saw Brophy tackle the other soldier in similar fashion, wrapping his thick arms around the man's throat.

In moments, both soldiers were unconscious.

Keegan let his man topple to the ground. He knelt and pulled a knife from the soldier's belt while Brophy and Lloyd grabbed the rifles. Keegan deftly flipped the blade around. In two quick motions, he severed the rope, freeing his wrists.

"Follow me," he said, and the trio fled toward the jungle.

19

2011

Sandy woke with a start.

In his dream, he'd been running. Trying to escape.

Only it had felt more like a memory than a dream.

He glanced around, half-expecting to see the dense darkness of the Central American jungle. Instead, the dirty metal dumpster filled his view. The stench of garbage followed a second later, snapping him back to reality.

The cold asphalt had seeped through the cardboard and into his bones, stiffening his joints as he moved. He shivered, even though a flush of warmth coated his skin.

I need to get this fever down.

He rose laboriously, suppressing a groan. He peered around the corner of the dumpster into the alleyway. He saw nothing out of place. The ambient noise of downtown at night filled his ears. He decided it was time to move.

Find a car.

Get the hell out of this town.

First, though, he removed his coat. He reached into his small day bag and pulled out a black shirt to replace the tan one he'd been wearing. Quickly, he changed into the new shirt. He debated swapping out the jeans as well, but the difference between the two pairs was minimal. Besides, he didn't want to take off his shoes.

He stuffed the old shirt back into the small bag. He double checked the compartments, removing the emergency cash he had stowed in an inner pocket. Then he lifted the black plastic lid of the dumpster and slipped the bag inside.

Sandy walked down the alley, working the kinks out of his muscles and joints. He'd switched from a blue baseball hat to a green knit cap, and from a tan shirt to a black one. He was no longer carrying a bag, either. It wasn't a massive change—his build was still the same, not to mention his hair and beard— but it might be enough to give anyone searching for him pause.

He could hope.

Just as he reached the mouth of the alley, a black and white patrol car turned the corner onto the street.

Shit.

So much for hope.

He turned to his left, walking casually in the same direction of travel as the vehicle. He hoped the cops would clock him as nothing out of the ordinary and drive right past. The level of diligence required to stop any and every person who vaguely resembled a particular suspect was high. And he'd modified his clothing, which might make for a quick rejection of him as a suspect.

Then again, he'd assaulted a pair of officers at the bus station. He knew neither would have been seriously injured from his actions. He also knew that wouldn't matter. Cops were a fraternal bunch by nature. An assault on any one of their own would motivate everyone to amp up their vigilance.

Just drive by.

The car swung to the curb, activating its overhead lights.

Sandy resisted the urge to immediately run. They were too close. If he ran while they were in the car, they had the advantage in keeping up with him. And they'd radio in the pursuit immediately. He knew all they were likely reporting now was a suspicious person stop. Maybe one more car would show up as backup but, until they were sure it was him, the cavalry wouldn't be coming.

So, he stopped, and waited.

A single officer exited the patrol car.

A woman.

She had an athletic build, reminding Sandy of a field hockey player or someone who competed in the strength-related track-and-field events. Her hair was drawn back in a tight bun. She moved with confidence but Sandy noted caution in her approach. Gun side away. Flashlight up at the left shoulder, shining in his face so he had to squint. She closed the distance but stopped just outside arm's reach.

Textbook.

"How's it going tonight?" she asked conversationally.

"Pretty good. You?"

"Oh, you know," she said. "Just working. Where you headed?"

"A bar, eventually. Kind of walking around till I see one that looks good." He shrugged. "It's a little dead out here."

She jerked her head to the west. "Most of the bars are that way."

"Oh. Thanks."

"No problem. Do you have any identification, sir?"

Sandy gave her a perplexed look. "Did I do something wrong?"

"Nope. Just want to know who I'm talking to, that's all."

He ran through his options in a millisecond, then decided on a course of action. "No problem." He reached for his wallet. "But afterward, maybe you can suggest the best bar within walking distance?"

"Sure. You from out of town?"

Sandy withdrew the wallet and opened it while he spoke. "I'm from Phoenix. Here for business."

"What kind of work do you do?"

He found his fake license in the name of Matthew Creighton and pulled it out. "I'm in sales," he said, holding it out for her.

"Selling what?"

"Siding. For houses."

The officer made a vague noise of comprehension and reached for the license. Sandy let go of it at the last possible second before her fingers clasped the thin plastic card. It fell downward, fluttering to the ground.

"Oh, sorry," he said, immediately.

The officer didn't stoop to retrieve it. He'd doubted she would, but it was worth an attempt. Feigning embarrassment, Sandy squatted down and picked it up. He handed it to her with a chagrined look. She took it and glanced down at the name.

"Matthew Creighton?"

"Yes, ma'am."

"What's your date of birth, sir?"

Sandy rattled off the date, one he'd committed easily to memory. It was Janet's birthday.

"How old are you?"

"Forty-six," he said. "For a little while longer, anyway."

The officer frowned slightly, glancing from the license photo to his bearded face. Sandy could sense she was torn between her instincts and the facts before her. He'd had the same experience in his years on the job. The gut says something is wrong, even though everything appears to be in order on the surface. An average or lazy cop wouldn't try to rectify that dissonance. Instead, she'd go with the facts—a solid ID, someone who knows their date of birth and age.

If she were a good cop—a diligent one—she'd dig a little deeper. She'd at least return to her car, check his name on the computer, wait for backup to arrive, and press further. It wouldn't take long to get past the walls he'd thrown up. Sure, Matthew Creighton's Arizona license was still good. There'd be no local record of him, since he wasn't from Minneapolis. But Sandy's physical appearance hadn't changed since the fight at the bus station, except for the shirt and the knit cap. No truly good cop would be convinced strictly based on that.

Did he look like a traveling salesman on his way to find a local bar? How much of the alley stink hung on him at this moment? How sick and disheveled did he look?

"Wait here," the officer said.

"Okay," he replied, trying to make his tone innocuous.

She took a step backward, then turned toward the vehicle. As soon as the apron of light left Sandy, he made his move. He shuffled forward quickly and whipping his rear leg around for a powerful kick. He targeted the outside thigh of her nearest leg.

The officer sensed his movement and started to shift to a defensive stance. He saw her right hand drop to the butt of her pistol just as his foot blasted into her thigh. Her leg buckled and she let out a guttural cry. At the same time, she surprised Sandy as she lashed out with the flashlight. The hard metal end struck him above the eye. He saw a flash of white while pain lanced through his head.

The blow stunned him briefly, long enough for the officer to come to rest on one knee and steady herself. She reached for her gun again. Sandy threw a straight left to her face. The punch caught her on the tip of the nose with a solid crunch. He jackhammered two more punches. The last one glanced off her forehead as she crumpled to the ground.

He didn't hesitate. Reaching down, he tore her portable radio from her belt. The cord leading to the microphone and ear-piece came free, whipping wildly in the air. Sandy flung the entire unit as far down the sidewalk as he could.

The officer groaned from the ground and turned on her side, pawing at her holster. Sandy grabbed her hand and twisted it into a wrist lock. In one smooth motion, he reached down and pulled her gun from the holster. Then he stood, letting go of her wrist. As he walked quickly toward the police car, he hit the magazine release. The fully loaded mag dropped out of the bottom of the weapon and clattered to the sidewalk. Sandy racked the slide, ejecting the round in the chamber. It flew up into the air, spinning and tumbling to the ground. Then he flung the gun away, too.

The door to the police cruiser was unlocked. Sandy got inside and closed the door. One of the buttons on the control panel was lit up with a red light and he punched it. Immediately, the overhead lights stopped, making the street far darker than it was moments ago.

On the sidewalk, he saw the officer struggling to her hands and knees.

He had only a little time before she alerted everyone.

He had to use it wisely.

Sandy dropped the vehicle into gear and chirped the tires as he pulled away.

20

1985
Nicaragua

Bullets chased them before they even reached jungle brush.

All three men ran straight ahead, weaving only slightly to throw off enemy aim. After the last ten yards, they plunged into the thick foliage. Rounds whistled and spat past them, slashing into trees and green growth. Keegan's shoeless feet stomped on the rough jungle floor. Adrenaline dulled the stabbing pain in his feet. Branches whipped across his arms, legs, and torso as he powered forward.

"Keep running," Keegan urged once, then saved his breath. Brophy and Lloyd kept at his heels, pausing only to return fire briefly. Lloyd's magazine ran dry, and he tossed the rifle aside. Brophy, ever the sniper, fired in controlled bursts every few yards. Then Keegan heard the distinctive clack that signaled the end of ammunition. He heard a muted clunk as Brophy let the weapon fall from his hands.

He leaned forward and sprinted harder.

Angry cries pursued them through the jungle night. At first, impossibly bright spotlights slashed through the darkness, searching for them. Other flashlights bounced in the blackness behind them like fishing bobbers atop the surface of a lake.

Keegan stumbled several times, once toppling to the jungle floor. He was forced to slow his pace and choose his route more carefully. The jungle floor bit at his bare feet. Vines, leaves, and bark scraped his arms and legs as he hurried past. He kept going, gritting his teeth against the pain. Brophy and Lloyd remained right behind him. He realized they were in single file and also clumped together within a grenade's radius.

"Fan out," he ordered. "Stay on my flanks."

The men obeyed immediately and they pushed forward.

The searchlights fell away as they made it deeper into the jungle, but the bobbing flashlights remained. So did the angry yells in Spanish. With every backward glance, Keegan realized they weren't increasing their lead on their pursuers. If anything, the Sandinistas were closing in.

It made sense. They knew this land far better than he and his men did. Even at night, this was an advantage. Plus, they were wearing boots and had light to assist them.

Just keep running west.

Get to the border.

Keegan staggered and almost fell.

Keep going. You owe these two men with you. And you made a promise to Janet.

Don't stop.

Keegan righted himself and kept his feet moving.

Long, frantic minutes passed with nothing but the sounds

of the jungle around him, the shouts of their pursuers, the occasional crack of a rifle, and his own labored breathing accenting their footfalls. Keegan's bare feet were heavy and throbbed in protest at the damage the jungle landscape was doing to them. He knew, once the adrenaline wore off, he'd be facing another round of pain.

If they survived, that was.

To his right, Brophy let out a pained cry.

Keegan waited a millisecond for the corresponding sound of a gunshot, but none came. "What is it?" he asked, slowing.

Brophy staggered forward and kept moving. "Goddamn snakebite, I think."

Shit.

Keegan's mind whipped through what he'd been briefed concerning local venomous snakes. In typical Army fashion, the simplistic explanation was, aside from a few species that were fairly rare, most of them could be generally compared to the U.S. rattlesnake.

"Not good to get bit by one," the medic had opined, "but not a death sentence, by any means. As long as it's not fer-delance or a coral snake, I've got anti-venom."

But Keegan didn't know what had bit Brophy.

"Did you see it?" he asked, as both men continued moving forward.

"Negative," came Brophy's strained reply.

Keegan's first inclination was to stop and examine the wound. But what could he tell from examining it, even if he could see well enough to do so?

No, their only chance was to keep driving north. Get to the border. Reunite with their unit so Brophy could get medical attention.

The problem was, every step they took caused Brophy's heart to beat harder. And every heartbeat spread the venom faster.

It was a Catch-22.

"I can make it," Brophy grunted, not slowing down beside him. "Hold the pace."

Keegan realized there was no choice. They'd make it or they wouldn't. Stopping, or even slowing down, was not an option.

"We're almost there," he said, though he wasn't entirely sure.

We have to be close.

They kept moving.

Despite their efforts, the lights behind them and the shouts grew nearer. Their trail was easy to follow. The Sandinistas knew they were making a beeline for the Honduras border. Keegan couldn't risk any evasive actions now. This wasn't a search for them to avoid. It was a race they needed to win.

"*Alla!*" An impossibly close shout rang out in jungle, then died on the dense foliage. A moment later, the shout was followed by a sputtering of rifle rounds. Bullets cut into the tree next to Keegan as he dropped into a crouch. To his left, Lloyd groaned. Keegan heard a loud thud as his companion collapsed to the ground.

"Evan!" Keegan kept his voice low.

On the other side of him, Brophy held up and waited, crouched behind the trunk of a tree.

"Evan!" Keegan repeated, more urgently.

Lloyd didn't reply.

Keegan turned to Brophy and waved him forward. "Keep going," he ordered.

"Sarge…"

In the darkness, he couldn't read Brophy's expression, but he could sense the hesitation in the man. "Move!" he said. "We'll be right behind you."

Brophy paused a moment, then turned and staggered forward.

Keegan slipped around the tree, staying low. He found Lloyd laying on his side. When he lowered his head, he heard the unmistakable gurgle of a sucking chest wound.

"Go…" Lloyd rasped wetly.

Keegan didn't answer. He took Lloyd by the arm and pulled him to a sitting position. Then he maneuvered him so he could execute a fireman's carry. With a grunt of exertion, he stood upward with Lloyd draped across his shoulders. His legs wavered under the weight but he ignored that. He turned and plodded heavily after Brophy. More shots trailed after him, whistling angrily past. Keegan didn't flinch. Instead, he focused on deep breaths and putting one foot in front of the other.

When he caught up to Brophy, he let the corporal remain in point position. They pushed steadily northwest, picking their way through the dense jungle. Keegan couldn't turn to see the lights behind them, but the shooting continued. The shots seemed random to him now, though, as if the pursuing soldiers had lost sight of the three of them.

They stumbled into a small clearing. At first, Keegan's heart fell. If they were spotted as they crossed the open space…

Then he saw it.

A road.

The road.

This was it. The border.

"Run," he urged Brophy.

The pair fell into an awkward, lumbering gait, hurrying for the woods along the far side of the road. Brophy swung his injured leg forward with each stride, almost a hitching gallop. Keegan stepped heavily, his throbbing feet stomping the ground as quickly as he could make them move. His lungs burned and he could taste blood. Evan's slack body bounced on his shoulders.

He didn't know if the Sandinistas would pursue them across the Honduran border or not. He doubted a line on the map would stop them. It hadn't mattered to them when they'd flanked his position earlier, so why would it matter now? Especially not if violating it meant recovering their prized American prisoners.

He couldn't control that.

All he could do was continue this stumbling run.

They kept moving. Keegan felt a small surge of elation when his feet dragged across the dirt road and they neared the cover of the bushes on the other side. He never imagined how good it would feel to be entering Honduras.

More voices. These were sharper now, not dampened by the surrounding jungle. They were in the clearing, too.

Angry shouts came next.

Shouts of discovery.

Then gunfire.

Concussive thuds rained down all around him. Keegan plunged into the bushes, following Brophy's lead. A broad leaf brushed across his head, suddenly covering the side of his face with warm wetness.

He continued.

This time, once they made it twenty meters into the cover of the jungle, Brophy angled northeast. This was the way back to the base camp, but it also took them out of the line of fire. As Keegan trudged along behind Brophy, he noticed the corporal's stumbling limp becoming more prominent. Behind them, the voices grew louder and the shooting continued. Most of the rounds poured into the jungle where they had been. A few strays whistled past them on this heading.

Keegan trudged onward.

Eventually, Brophy's stride deteriorated into a near stagger. He slowed and limped painfully with each hopping step. The stubborn soldier refused to stop, and Keegan matched his pace, ever forward.

Soon he noticed the noise from the Sandinistas grew more distant. He realized they had stopped at the border, despite his misgivings. Maybe there was an officer in command instead of a sergeant. Someone who weighed losing these prisoners against the risk of an international incident an armed incursion in Honduras might cause. Keegan didn't know. Whatever the reason, that decision was the first piece of good luck they'd experienced so far on this mission.

"They're not coming," Keegan said with labored breaths. "Come on. We just have to make base camp. That's all."

That's all, he mused. The base camp was an hour and a half away. Worse yet, that hour and a half trek was in daylight, with boots, guided by Contras who knew the route. Not two barefoot men in the dark, one snake-bit and the other carrying a third.

How long did Lloyd have before he bled out?

Or Brophy, before the venom took hold?

I can't think that way.

We're all going to make it.

Push forward.

Keegan swallowed a deep breath and kept moving.

Twenty minutes later, when the three of them were suddenly awash in lights, he stopped in exhausted resignation. His first thought was the Sandinistas had fooled him. They'd looped around and took an alternate route through the jungle to get ahead of them and cut off their escape. He blinked against the glare, waiting for the inevitable.

"*Americanos,*" breathed someone in surprise.

Then the lights dropped out of his eyes. He recognized first the uniform, then one of the faces.

Contras.

The face he recognized took a moment to register. Then it came to him.

Lieutenant Blandon.

Ernesto.

Keegan collapsed to his knees and eased Lloyd to the ground. "He needs a medic," he said, his voice hoarse and ragged. Then he motioned to Brophy. "And he's snake-bit."

Blandon barked a few rapid orders in Spanish. A pair of medics sprang into action. The lieutenant came closer to Keegan while one medic knelt to examine Lloyd.

"Donde esta Sergeante Aguilar?" he asked.

Keegan answered without looking up. "Dead," he told Blandon. *"Muerto."*

"Serio?" Lieutenant Blandon asked him.

Keegan met his gaze. "Yes," was all he said.

Blandon's jaw flexed, but he didn't react otherwise. He pointed to Keegan's face. *"Mucha Sangre,"* he said.

Keegan lifted his hand to where the wet leaf had brushed across his face. His fingers pressed into the tacky blood there. He pulled his hand away, a sinking feeling settling into his stomach.

The medic looked up from Lloyd's still body. *"Él también,"* he said.

Keegan stared at him in disbelief.

The medic glanced at Blandon, then back to Keegan. Then he shook his head and repeated, *"Muerto."*

"I fucking understood you." Keegan choked out the words. He dropped his gaze down to Lloyd's motionless body.

How far had he carried a dead man?

It didn't matter, he decided. They didn't leave him behind. That was what mattered.

If anything mattered at all, that was.

***

At base camp, doctors treated their wounds. Keegan's body was laced with cuts and bruises. His feet were swollen, a web of carved slashes and punctures. He sat on the edge of the cot, soaking them in sterilization fluid, wrapped in a blanket.

Nearby, Brophy groaned and shuddered. The doctors had washed the wound and given him anti-venom. He lay on his back, his leg off the side of the cot, resting on a pillow.

It was a waiting game now for the corporal. Keegan caught enough of the doctor's quasi-coded speech to understand the situation. If the snake that bit Brophy was one of the species comparable to a rattlesnake, he would survive. They'd discussed the possibility of amputation but neither doctor thought it likely.

But if the bite had been a fer-de-lance or a coral snake… it was only a matter of time before his friend succumbed to the venom.

"Where's Lloyd?" Brophy asked through gritted teeth.

"They took care of him," Keegan told him.

Brophy didn't answer. He turned to his side and retched into the bedpan the nurse left for him.

"Tranquilo," the nurse said.

Brophy finished retching and spat. Keegan noticed he was shivering. Despite that, he glanced up at the small Contra woman in fatigues. "Senorita, I am the furthest goddamn thing from *tran-kwilo.*"

Lieutenant Culliver tried to debrief Keegan that first night, but the doctors put him off. Normally, he would have waved aside their concerns. But he didn't want to leave Brophy's side while the man battled for his life. And if he was honest with himself, he didn't want to relive the events yet. So he turned onto his side and went to sleep.

The next day, he awoke early. In the cot next to him, Brophy slept fitfully. His breathing was shallow but constant. Keegan looked over at the nurse on duty. She was older than the woman from last night, her expression harder.

"He's okay?" Keegan asked.

The woman shrugged. "He is still alive," she said in a stilted accent.

"He'll make it, then?"

She gave him a short nod. *"Creo que sí."*

Keegan let out a long breath of relief. He reached out and patted the sleeping corporal on the shoulder. Then he glanced around for his clothing.

"What do you need?" the nurse asked.

"My clothes," he said. He looked down at his bandaged feet. "And some extra-large socks."

The nurse didn't move right away. She seemed to be considering his request. After a while, though, she rose and left the medical tent. A while later, she returned with the clothing Keegan requested. The uniform was his spare one. It fit easily enough, but dressing took him a long time. Every muscle in his body screamed with soreness with each motion he took. Even sliding the buttons into their respective holes hurt his fingers.

The socks and boots were not his. Both looked like FDN issue. He carefully eased his bandaged feet into the large woolen socks. Then he slid into a pair of unlaced boots several sizes bigger than his own. He made a loose bow knot to keep the laces from trailing on the ground. Then he stood up, wincing.

"You need more rest," the nurse told him, her tone bland.

He ignored the advice. Instead, he shuffled along toward the exit. Before ducking under the tent flap, he glanced over at her. *"Gracias,"* he said.

"De nada."

Keegan shuffled carefully across the base camp toward his destination. When he reached Lieutenant Culliver's command tent, he stopped just outside. In a strange moment of dissonance, he realized he didn't have his cover. He ran a hand over his bare head. His shoulder muscles sang in protest at the motion. At the same time, his chest felt empty and bare. He didn't care he was out of uniform.

It didn't matter.

All that mattered was Evan Lloyd was dead. Brophy was alive but maimed. And it was his fault. He made the decision that caused it all.

Keegan raised his hand. He slapped his palm against the canvas tent. "Sir?" he called. "Permission to enter?"

"Come," said Culliver, from inside.

Keegan pushed aside the flap and stepped through the opening. Lieutenant Culliver stood next to his field desk, examining a map. He glanced up at Keegan. Culliver's eyes narrowed, but he said nothing as Keegan shuffled closer.

Finally, when Keegan was an arm's length away, he stopped. He drew himself up to the position of attention, his eyes straight ahead.

"Sir," he said, his voice falling into a formal, staccato rhythm. "Sergeant Fuller, reporting for debrief, sir."

Culliver watched him for a few moments. Then he said, "Very well, Sergeant. Tell me how in the hell this clusterfuck came to pass."

Keegan didn't move. "Sir, it was my fault," was all he said.

Lieutenant Culliver waved for him to continue.

Keegan told him everything.

21

2011

Special Agent Carter stared at Danforth for a long while after she'd finished. Despite her earlier protestations, she was stunned. Not just at the events themselves, nor the matter of fact fashion in which the intelligence agent—or whatever the hell Danforth was—recounted them. Both were reason enough for surprise but, perhaps more than anything else, she was stunned he openly shared the information with her at all.

Finally, she found her voice. "So, what happened? Since this is the first time I'm hearing about these events, there obviously wasn't an international incident."

"No," said Danforth. "There wasn't."

"Bet that took some doing."

"My understanding is it involved considerable effort and finesse." Danforth smiled humorlessly. "But that is our forte."

Carter didn't react to his hubris. Instead, she waved for him to continue.

Danforth seemed unperturbed. "The Nics tried to float a protest with the international community. All they had were a pair of dog tags to back up their claims. We made sure those tags didn't carry any weight."

"How?"

"Lloyd was already dead," Danforth explained. "His official duty station, like Fuller and Brophy, was Fort Benning. So we manufactured a training accident that sadly took the lives of PFC Evan Lloyd and Sergeant Keegan Fuller."

"What kind of accident?"

"The training kind," Danforth replied wanly. Then he shrugged. "It involved explosives during a breaching operation. Neither soldier suffered."

Carter thought about it. Then she said, "Pretty big coincidence, isn't it? The both of them dying right at the same time the Nicaraguans are claiming they captured them?"

"One could argue the Nicaraguans were being opportunistic."

"But they somehow chose those two soldiers? *And* they have their dog tags?" Carter turned over her hands. "Seems like compelling evidence."

"It's not," Danforth assured her. "Nicaraguan intelligence was capable of getting that information. They weren't on par with us or the Soviets at the time, but there were still a lot of connections that remained from the Somoza days. Access to details about a tragic training accident wouldn't be difficult. It was entirely plausible they mined the intelligence and then created this fiction of capturing the soldiers from it, fully intending to use the training accident itself as proof of a cover-up."

"Which it was."

Danforth ignored her. "As for the dog tags…?" He shook

his head. "Anyone can manufacture realistic ones. Hollywood does it for every war movie."

"I still think the timing is suspect. I'm surprised this didn't get any traction."

Danforth's humorless smile broadened. "The timing is exactly why it didn't. You see, the deaths of Lloyd and Fuller at Fort Benning occurred a full six weeks before the supposed incursion incident in Nicaragua."

Carter took a moment to process the information. She saw how that could work, especially since Banks—*Keegan,* she reminded herself—didn't have any family connections. But what about Evan Lloyd?

"How'd you manage that?" she asked. "I don't imagine Lloyd's parents were too pleased to hear how their son died and they weren't notified for six weeks."

"That also took some finesse," Danforth admitted. "In the end, they were convinced the need for a thorough investigation took precedence. Besides, they were a patriotic couple, and their son was given a hero's funeral."

"All the loose ends nicely sewn up," Carter said. "Impressive."

"Damage control is what it was."

"What about Keegan Fuller? He couldn't stay in the military, being dead and all."

Danforth opened his mouth to reply, but Carter cut him off.

"Dead for the second time," she said.

Danforth tilted his head and waited.

"I know that before Keegan Fuller enlisted in the Army, he died of whooping cough at the age of three," Carter told him. "The military must have been pretty desperate, signing up a zombie."

That brought a bare smile to Danforth's lips. "Nice work, Agent Carter. Let's put a pin in that for just a few moments longer."

Carter shrugged. She wanted to push Danforth for more relevant, current information. But she was curious about the fallout from the events in Nicaragua. So, she waited.

"With Fuller and Lloyd both deceased," continued Danforth, "the rumblings from the Sandinistas were lost in the midst of all the other political chatter of the time. Stories with more compelling evidence, or just more scandalous assertions, came along and sucked out all the oxygen from this story. It fell to the wayside and is mostly lost to history.

"As for the soldiers involved, since the Nics didn't have Corporal Brophy's identity, he was allowed to retire medically. Evan Lloyd, as I mentioned, was given a military burial. And Keegan Fuller was given a new identity."

"The third identity of his life," Carter observed.

"True, though no one knew that at the time. My understanding is he was allowed to choose his new name. For whatever reason, he picked Sandy Banks. A military jacket was created for him under this new name, and he was given an honorable discharge and released from service. From there, he went on to have a police career in Spokane, Washington, and… well, you know the rest, don't you?"

"In exceeding detail," Carter said. "So, let's change gears and talk about now. This guy I know as Banks—who was Fuller, and someone unknown before that—where is he going?"

"Tennessee, we hope. Eventually. Don't get me wrong—if the locals in Minneapolis can apprehend him, that would be a pleasant turn of events. But, as you no doubt saw in Spokane, Banks is a slippery individual."

"That's one word for it." Carter pursed her lips. "Tennessee doesn't exactly narrow it down. Just because his fake identity came from there…" She trailed off as Danforth smirked at her. "What?"

"You found out Keegan Fuller died at three," he said. "That was excellent investigative work. I'll go you one better. One of my colleagues located a small operation in the region that has specialized in creating false identities for decades. We passed the information on to your agency, in fact." He raised a brow. "Your colleagues raided the place since they were making licenses from multiple states. Multiple suspects were arrested. Several went to prison. A couple were given suspended sentences and hired by the company as consultants. All in all, that made it pretty easy to trace the sale of the Keegan Fuller identity."

Carter took it all in. Her posting was in Spokane, so it made sense to her that a raid on a fraud operation in Tennessee wouldn't stick in her mind. The self-important tone in Danforth's voice bothered her, though, as well as the way he seemed to revel in telling her how he manipulated her own agency.

"Who bought the identity?"

Danforth raised a finger. "We're not quite to that point of the story yet, Agent Carter. Let's focus on the *where* before the *who*."

"Fine," she said briskly. "*Where* is he going now? As in, *exactly*."

"Truthfully, we haven't narrowed it down to a single location yet."

"How far have you narrowed it?"

"A town," Danforth said. "A specific, *small* town."

"What's the name?"

Danforth shifted a little uncomfortably in his seat. "We're not entirely certain he'll go there," he backtracked.

"Yes, you are."

"Agent Carter—"

"He thought his Keegan Fuller identity was solid enough to go to Evan Lloyd's grave site," she said. "If he believes his true identity can't be connected to Fuller's, where else would he go but home?"

"There are other considerations," Danforth said.

"Tell me what they are."

He paused. "If I tell you, there's a condition."

"Aw, Jesus," she muttered. "There's always a condition with you people."

"That's the third time you've used that term," Danforth said, his tone unperturbed. "You should really be careful. It's long been considered potentially racist."

"I meant spooks and you know it."

Danforth looked at her pointedly.

"What?" she asked.

"Am I to believe you're unaware of the multiple meanings of *that* word?" Danforth asked. An amused smirk crossed his face. "If I didn't know better, I'd think you were flinging left-handed insults my way."

"Believe me," Carter said. "When I insult you, it'll be intentional. You won't miss it. Now, what's your condition?"

Danforth's placid expression returned. "It isn't an onerous one."

She waved for him to continue.

"When you find him," Danforth said, "you call me first."

"That's it?"

"Yes. And I do mean *first*. You call me before you book him, before you even tell your boss." He paused a beat, then added, "I get to interview him before you take him away."

"What do you want from him?"

Danforth shook his head. "You don't need to know that. You just need to get me my face time with him. In primary position."

"Why don't *you* just act on it? Put your own people on it?"

"Come now, Agent Carter. You know we don't work that

way. My resources are smaller than you think. More importantly, our role is clandestine in nature. By law, the CIA can't operate on domestic soil."

"I know, but—"

"My unit can't operate anywhere. Because we don't exist. Are you understanding me?"

She nodded slowly. "All right. But why use me at all?"

"It's simple. You have access to easier, more public resources. You can operate out in the open. Your efforts can be noticed. Your results are not extralegal."

She shook her head. "You're manipulating me. You want to use me."

Danforth clapped his hands together slowly several times. "Congratulations, Agent Carter. I just told you that. Now, do you want the deal or not?"

She stared at him. Imagined finally slipping handcuffs over the wrists of Sandy Banks. If all it took was to allow this arrogant bastard to have a few words with him first, it was worth it.

"Fine," she snapped. "Tell me the rest."

22

Sandy pulled the police car into a metered parking stall. He shut it down, got out, and walked away without looking back. He'd driven the vehicle for less than a minute, heading in one direction to put some distance between himself and the officer he'd been forced to subdue.

Subdue? You beat the shit out of her.

He pushed the thought away. He'd done the same at the bus station when he blasted both officers with the sap. It wasn't something he enjoyed, but it had been necessary for his survival.

Foot traffic picked up substantially as he walked east. Sandy took advantage of the camouflage to duck into a drug store. He grabbed some Tylenol and moved to the register. The clerk, a rotund man in a Minnesota Twins jersey, punched at the keys.

"Just coming from the game?" he asked amiably.

"What?"

"Twins game?" the man asked. "Season finale? Baseball?"

"Oh." Sandy shook his head. "No, just out for a walk."

"Well, you missed a dandy. Two outs, scoreless in the bottom of the ninth, and Plouffe jacks a double to send Span home." He glanced at the register and gave Sandy the cost of the Tylenol. Sandy handed him a bill. "Kept us from losing a hundred games this year," the clerk continued, as the cash drawer popped open. He made change and extended it toward Sandy. "It's not the pennant, but sometimes ya gotta take what good you can, am I right?"

"You're right," Sandy agreed.

He accepted the cash and slid the coins into a small tray near the register for those needing to make exact change.

"Next season will be better," the clerk said.

"I hope so."

"Have a good one."

Sandy nodded to him and left the store. Outside, he opened the box as he walked and dry-swallowed two capsules. More pedestrians filled the sidewalk. When he turned a corner, he saw a baseball stadium several blocks away from which most of the foot traffic was spilling out onto the street. Sandy paused and watched the flow for a minute or so. While he did, he noticed several police cars near the stadium. Officers were out on foot, half-heartedly directing the crowd.

He didn't want to get any closer. Maybe the officers on the traffic control detail wouldn't be hyper-aware, but he didn't want to risk it. He glanced up at the nearest street sign, which read Hennepin Avenue. Further down the pole was a sign for the metro, along with an arrow. Pedestrians streamed that direction.

Sandy joined the flow. As he walked, he considered his decision. The metro line could get him out of the downtown area quickly. It was also likely to be well-covered with cameras and transit police if Minneapolis went the route most cities did. Those transit cops would have received his description by now. They'd be looking for him.

He kept walking, working it out in his head.

They'd be looking for him in a sea of people. He had a different hat, a different shirt, and wasn't carrying a bag. In the mass of humanity, a cop's gaze might skip right over him.

Unless the last cop updated his description which she was sure to do.

He couldn't help that now. The bigger concern was, if they spotted him on the metro, he was in a contained location. Escape would be difficult, if not impossible. Entering the metro car was an all-in proposition; he got away or he got caught.

He decided to chance it.

At the entrance, he stood in a brief line to buy a one way ticket from one of the dispensers along a wall. Most passengers must have bought round trip tickets earlier or had passes, so the line went quickly. Sandy chose the blue line, paying for a ticket that took him all the way to the Mall of America. Then he inserted it into the turnstile and entered the station. He joined the thick flow of passengers, trying to blend in.

He spotted the first transit officer as he came around a corner near the entrance to the platform. The man stood stoically, surveying the crowd. Sandy didn't sense any particular urgency from him but avoided looking directly at him all the same. He kept to the middle of the crowd and stood facing the empty space where the train would hopefully be soon. A digital timer hung from the ceiling and counted down from just under two minutes, signifying the arrival of the next car.

Sandy imagined the transit officer's gaze burning into the back of his head. In his peripheral vision, he checked the timer. Was ninety seconds long enough for him to call for back up if he made an identification? Or could he delay the train itself in order to apprehend Sandy? Would he make the attempt alone?

The entire thought process felt alien to him. He'd experienced the same strangeness in Spokane once everything had gone off the rails. It was weird to him to be at odds with the police after being an officer himself for so many years. Sure, during his time as a Horseman, he had to account for avoiding the cops. Somehow, that always felt like it was for their own good, so they weren't forced to undo the justice he was bringing to bear.

Justice, he mused. That was arguable. Even if every terrible person he took down was a form of justice, the death of an innocent woman at the end counter-balanced much of that justice. So did the round he put into Agent Scott McNichol's thigh. All of his actions after that seemed to put his karmic balance into the negative.

The train whooshed into the stop. The doors slid open. Only a few people exited the partially full train. Sandy pressed forward, managing to be one of the last to make it on before a beep signaled the doors closing. The train lurched forward.

Sandy stood, his gaze cast downward while he held onto a silver pole. As the train rumbled down the track, he wondered about justice. He'd brought the hard hammer of justice down on so many bad men in his life, including his own stepfather. But that first time had been more about vengeance than justice, hadn't it? Were the rest the same?

Had it all been some kind of selfish act on his part?

Sandy swallowed and rubbed his eyes with his free hand. He didn't have time for these thoughts. He needed to focus. He needed a plan.

At each stop, more passengers exited than got on the train. By the time he reached the Mall of America, the train was only half-full. Even so, no transit police had come through the car he was in. Relieved to be free of those close confines, Sandy exited onto the platform. He ignored the posted officer who stood nearby, giving directions to a pretty woman with a young boy in tow.

Two minutes later, he was out of the station.

Sandy walked as if he were headed to his own car. When he discovered an older model with a window cracked open, he used a combination of force and finesse to pop the door lock. Less than two minutes later, he had the engine started. Sandy pulled out of the parking lot and drove at a leisurely pace, following traffic to the freeway. When he saw a sign for Chicago, he glanced at the fuel gauge, which sat at three quarters.

It was enough. Maybe one pit stop for gas.

Sandy took the on-ramp. He had to get clear of this heat and lose any possibility of a tail before he headed to Tennessee.

Before he went home.

23

"**M**ayford Sutter," Danforth said. "That's the man who bought the Keegan Fuller identity."

Agent Carter let the name wash over her. "That's who Sandy Banks used to be?"

"No, though we thought so at first. But it was obvious early on that Mayford was too old."

"Father?"

"A cousin, actually. He lives in the sticks outside a very small town known as—and get this—Big Sandy, Tennessee."

Carter smirked in disbelief. "You've got to be kidding me."

"I am not. Anyway, we started looking into Mayford's family tree. It took a little while to piece it together but, eventually, we came across his first cousin, William Sutter. The two were around the same age, but William died in 1970."

"How?"

"Accidental," Danforth said. "He worked at a hydraulics

manufacturing plant. A piece of machinery broke away and clocked him in the head."

Carter twirled her finger impatiently. "He had a son or something…?"

"He did. Willam A. Sutter, Junior."

"And that's who Sandy Banks was?"

"We believe so."

"What makes you think that?"

"After his father's death, his mother, Eileen Sutter, remarried less than a year later. The stepfather—a man named Errol Shelton—worked on and off at an auto parts plant. From what we can tell, he was abusive toward both Eileen and young William. Also, Errol and Eileen apparently drank rather heavily, which I'm sure only exacerbated that behavior."

"I think I see where this is going."

"No doubt you do. Eileen Sutter died of heart failure in 1982. Two days after her funeral, Errol Shelton's body was discovered. His throat was slashed and he'd been stabbed multiple times. And young William Sutter was missing."

"He blamed the stepfather for his mother's death," murmured Carter thoughtfully.

"Apparently so."

"Where's the trail pick up from there?"

"It doesn't. It ends. To this day, William A. Sutter, Junior remains missing. The Benton County Sheriff's Office has an outstanding arrest warrant for him, but the investigation is in a drawer somewhere. We got the strong sense no one put a ton of effort into finding the young man back then and are even less interested now. Seems most folks saw it as a man getting what he deserved." Danforth gave her a pointed look. "As justice."

"That explains a lot."

"In a way, I suppose it does. Nevertheless, here we are, more than a quarter century later, piecing things together.

Our reconstruction has Mayford Sutter procuring the Keegan Fuller paperwork for young William, who promptly went to Memphis and enlisted in the military."

Carter shook her head, frowning. "It was that easy to get in?"

"Easy?" Danforth shrugged. "He had his birth certificate and a school identification card. A valid social security number. He went infantry. No security clearance necessary. Just a little paperwork and a willing mindset."

Carter took in a deep breath and let it out. She glanced out the window to see they were pulling onto the airfield road. "All right, so what did this guy Mayfield have to say?"

"Mayford," corrected Danforth. "Nothing, unfortunately. We have been unable to locate his cabin in the woods."

"Seriously?"

"Yes. He has a mail box at the Big Sandy post office, but no physical address listed anywhere. The locals have been unsurprisingly less than helpful in pointing the way."

"In an entire town, there's no one with an axe to grind? Someone who might know the location?" Carter found that difficult to believe.

"There are fewer than five hundred souls in Big Sandy," said Danforth. "If any of them take issue with Mayford Sutter, it isn't serious enough to outweigh their distrust and/or dislike for federal agents."

"Great," muttered Carter. She knew clannish tendencies were difficult to crack.

She sat quietly, thinking about all the intelligence agent had shared with her on this ride to the airport. The car exited the road into a parking lot. Instead of stopping, the driver took a small access road to the edge of the tarmac, where he stopped. A small jet stood on the airstrip, the passenger door open and a set of portable stairs wheeled up tight.

"Of course, all of this is just history, isn't it?" Danforth said. "We can't know Sandy Banks is going home. It's just our best guess. Without knowing for certain, or even why he might make the trip—"

"I think I can help with that," Carter said, interrupting him. "I found the remnants of a note in his belongings, four months ago. The note was brief but, in it, he said he was coming home."

Danforth's brow shot up. "That wasn't in your reports, Agent Carter."

"It's an ongoing investigation."

The CIA agent didn't appear convinced, but he didn't push the matter. "Banks wrote he was coming home, you said?"

Carter nodded.

"And who was this letter addressed to?"

"A woman."

"Would you care to be more specific?"

"I'll tell you," Carter said. "But if we miss him in Minneapolis, I'll need you to get me to Tennessee."

Danforth's smile was almost genuine. "Where do you think this plane is going? The flight plan has already been filed to Memphis. Your little informant, Moore, is on board. Under guard, of course."

"But—"

"I'll see you're notified if Banks is apprehended in Minneapolis," Danforth said. "Meanwhile, why don't we start approaching this pro-actively instead reactively? Perhaps end this, once and for all?"

Carter felt a burn of irritation in her chest at his words. She opened her mouth to reply, but Danforth cut her off.

"Go to Big Sandy, Agent Carter," he said. His smooth voice had a hard edge to it. "Set the trap."

24

When Sandy crossed the northern border of Tennessee on Sunday, a twinge of nostalgia rippled through him.

I am almost home.

He didn't know if Janet had stayed in Big Sandy, or what her life was like. All he knew for certain was he would finally fulfill his promise to her. What happened after that was a future unwritten.

He drove a blue Ford Escort he'd stolen in Evansville from a used car lot. The sign outside proudly proclaimed "Closed on the Sabbath" which Sandy took as a blessing. He took a chance the office wasn't alarmed or that it tripped silent. The back door wasn't difficult to force and he was greeted with silence on the other side. Quickly, he pulled a random key from the board, reading the tag that hung from it. The tag read *Ford Esc*, followed by a license plate.

Sandy located the blue car in less than thirty seconds. Fifteen seconds later, he was on the road again. He knew, if it had been alarmed, it'd be at least an hour before the police would be able to get an owner to respond and determine which car was missing. By then he'd be out of the reach of local law enforcement. As long as he didn't give the state patrol or any other cops a reason to check his license plate, he should be safe. Besides, the remaining leg of his journey was only about three hours' worth of driving.

The closer he got to Big Sandy, the more anticipation built inside him. The emotion rose up even as his fever diminished. To be safe on that front, he popped another dosage of Tylenol into his mouth while he drove. He focused on forcing himself calm. He was still on the run. Any casual encounter with police could end in catastrophe. Only now, the risk was increased. Not only was he a fugitive as Sandy Banks, but someone locally might recognize him as William Sutter, Junior. He was confident there was still some kind of warrant for him regarding the murder of Errol Shelton.

Sandy's jaw twitched. Calling Errol's death a murder burned in his gut.

That had been justice.

Of that, he was sure.

It had been vengeance, and justice.

That fact and his promise to Janet, were the only two beliefs of which he remained certain.

That didn't change the fact the cops in Benton County, Tennessee, would be very interested in laying hands on William Sutter *or* Sandy Banks. So, he kept his car at the speed limit. The Indiana plates weren't ideal, but he wanted to believe they were less of a ticket target than they might have been when he left almost three decades ago. Certainly, they were less inviting to a patrol cop than plates out of Chicago.

He passed a sign that told him Big Sandy was ten miles

away. Shortly after that, he found the side road that took him toward Mayford's cabin. After a ten-minute drive, he slowed, watching for the large ash tree near the road. A barely used access road had been there years ago. Sandy didn't know what to expect now. Things could have changed significantly since he was last here. Much of the land was BLM but some belonged to the county. Maybe someone developed the land and he'd find a paved thoroughfare.

But the land to his left and right remained largely unchanged despite the passage of time. A few homes dotted the countryside, none of them very new. The nagging sense of a near memory hung over Sandy when it came to most of them.

In the end, he drove past the large ash tree and had to backtrack. It had been cut back severely and resembled more of an over-sized stump than the majestic tree it once was. But Sandy was able to make out twin ruts of the vague access road, barely visible in the weedy growth.

This could be it.

He turned off the county road. Foliage raked the underside of the small car as he drove slowly along the bumpy roadway. After fifty yards or so, the road disappeared into the woods. Only a narrow passageway between two trees existed. Sandy eased the car through. He drove a short distance further but, as soon as he spotted an area off the roadway large enough to fit the car, he swung the wheel that direction. He parked about ten yards off the roadway and got out. The canopy of foliage above the car was thick and he gathered more and covered it almost completely.

His reasons for leaving the car behind were simple. For one, he didn't know if the car could make the rest of the trip. Mayford always owned a truck to traverse the rugged pathway. More than that, though, he didn't want to approach Mayford's cabin in an unknown vehicle. There was no way to know how his older cousin would react. The man had been a little paranoid and anti-government before. Sandy doubted the years had tempered that outlook.

On the flip side, if he was somehow being followed or tracked due to the vehicle, he didn't want to lead the Feds any closer. The chances were slim at this point but, if all Sandy had to do was walk a few miles in order to negate them, it was worth it.

He started hiking, following the faint twin ruts that quickly resembled more of an animal trail than a road. The forest floor off the pathway was littered with dried leaves and broken twigs. The strong aroma of eastern red cedars filled his nose, along with an undercurrent he couldn't quite define. Perhaps it was the mountain laurels or some other trees injecting some small element into the scent. The result was the unique smell of the Smoky Mountains.

The smell of home.

Sandy smiled sadly and continued walking.

After about two miles, the makeshift road ended at a clearing. Sandy stood at the edge, hesitating. It occurred to him Mayford was the kind of person who may have resorted to booby-trapping the area near his cabin. There'd been a couple he'd told Sandy about while he was hiding out with him after Errol's death. Could there be more now?

He decided on the most direct route to where he recalled the cabin was. As he trudged across the open field, he kept his head up and his face visible. He hoped Mayford wouldn't simply shoot on sight. Or if that response was his default, he'd at least take a look at his face before cranking off a round. But there was no telling for certain.

The slight trepidation in his stomach brought back memories of that fateful flight through the central American jungle all those years ago.

He pushed away the thought and kept on.

When he reached the edge of the clearing without incident, he breathed a small sigh of relief and slipped into the trees again. He could smell the faint odor of smoke. It wasn't far now.

A few minutes later, he was greeted by the outline of Mayford's cabin amongst the trees. It looked almost exactly the same, as if it had been preserved in time. The only difference he saw at first glance was a metal roof, and even that was worn and faded.

Sandy took a step forward.

"That'll be far enough," a voice rasped from behind a nearby tree.

Sandy stopped. He lifted his hands slowly and turned his face toward the sound. All he could see from his angle was the long barrel of a shotgun along the side of the tree. The hole at the end of the barrel looked massive.

"Easy," he said. "Cousin Mayford, it's me."

There was a silence. Sandy could hear the distant chatter of a squirrel and the coo of a bird while he waited. Finally, Mayford asked, "How do you know my name?"

"It's me," Sandy repeated. "Will. Your cousin."

Another silence. Then Mayford let out a low exhale that whistled through his teeth. "I'll be damned," he muttered.

The gun barrel lowered. A much older, slightly shrunken version of his Cousin Mayford stepped out from behind the tree. A smile creased his lined face. "Goddamn, son. It's really you."

Sandy stepped forward and embraced him. The man's funk caught in his throat, but he didn't care. The rush of emotion as he clung to his only surviving relative surprised Sandy. He held the embrace much longer than he intended.

Mayford patted his back with his free hand, holding the shotgun to the side. "It's good to see you, too, boy," he whispered huskily.

Sandy broke the embrace and stepped back. He cleared his throat and tried to reply. Tears choked him again, and he stopped. Unable to speak, he nodded his head in agreement.

Mayford looked him up and down as he flopped the shotgun barrel into the crook of his arm. "Damn," he said. "You got old, Will."

Sandy burst into laughter.

After a moment, Mayford joined him, chuckling. When their laughter faded, he asked, "Why are you here? You know you're still wanted over that one son of a bitch, right?" Mayford turned to the side and spat.

Sandy noticed he didn't use Errol's name. "I'm sure that's true. But I need your help."

Mayford eyed him for a moment. "Yeah?"

Sandy nodded. "Yeah."

"Well, then," Mayford said, jerking his head in the direction of the cabin. "Come on. Let's get ourselves a drink and figure this out."

25

Agent Lori Carter rolled along the main thoroughfare of Big Sandy, Tennessee, in her rental car.

She was anxious, but in a good way. It felt like pre-game jitters she'd experienced before a game when she'd played volleyball in both high school and college. Part nerves, part anticipation.

They were getting close. She could feel it. While Brian Moore was safely ensconced at the Memphis Field Office, she did legwork here in Big Sandy. For his part, Danforth had arranged for an aerial search of the woodlands surrounding the town. While no one at the Sheriff's Office claimed to know exactly where Mayford Sutter's cabin was, she'd managed to get one deputy to suggest a compass direction.

"North," he said. "Maybe."

It wasn't much to go on. Nonetheless, Danforth's allies at NSA redirected a drone flight over the area. The intent was to identify any likely targets from the air then investigate on foot. Her own boss, Special-Agent-in-Charge (SAC) Maw had made the necessary calls to have a tactical team dispatched to the region under her command.

She half-expected the SAC to come out himself. He was a notorious glory hound. Capturing Banks would be a feather in his cap. Then again, she realized, he'd still get some credit when she made the arrest. That was the nature of bureaucracy. Bosses got credit for what their people did.

By *not* coming out on the operation, though, Maw created a little distance in the event all of this effort ended up in a giant swing-and-a-miss. He could blame her and keep his own reputation intact. It was the safest move and a career-long administrator like him knew it.

Carter pushed aside thoughts of her supervisor and glanced out the car window. The town she saw was more than small; in the area of New England where she grew up, people might even call it a village. Still, the basics of communal existence were clearly present. Food, supplies, entertainment. Road infrastructure that was surprisingly new. Carter suspected federal dollars had paid for that.

She'd already been to what was once the Sutter residence, a yellow, recently painted house on the edge of town. Winona, a young woman with her toddler at her knee, answered when Carter knocked.

"Never heard of any Sutters," she told Carter. She patted the toddler's head. "Then again, I've been busy with her."

"How long have you lived here?" Carter asked.

"Let's see. Tanya was six months old when we bought the place, so… a little over a year and a half now."

"What brought you to Big Sandy?"

"Work," Winona said, brushing a lock of hair from her forehead. Next to her, little Tanya clung to her mother's leg and stared up at Carter. "My husband's a teacher. We used to live in Memphis, but he grew up in a small town and always wanted to teach in one, so when he found this job…" She raised her hands and dropped them. "Well, here we are."

"Has anyone you don't know come by the house?" Carter asked.

"You mean like a salesman? Or Jehovies? Because we don't truck with those oddball religions. We're Baptists."

Carter showed her a smile she didn't feel. "No, not like that. More along the lines of someone who may have once lived here."

Winona looked confused but shook her head. "No, ma'am. Is that something I ought to worry about?"

"No." Carter withdrew her business card from her wallet and extended it toward her. "All the same, if anything odd happens, give me a call."

Winona accepted the card reluctantly. "All right."

"You have a good day," Carter said.

"You, too," Winona replied, looking down at the card. "Sorry I couldn't be more helpful."

"Actually," said Carter, "you've helped me out a lot."

She had. The mention of her husband being a teacher fast-tracked the idea of where she should check next. After she drove through what passed for a downtown core of the small town, she sought out the high school. At first, she worried the high school students in Big Sandy were bused to a larger community. Then she spotted a small sign to the high school and followed the road there.

The school looked like any of a hundred others she'd seen. Blocky architecture dotted with open grassy areas. In the distance, a pair of football goal posts bracketed a gridiron. "Home of the Red Devils!" along with a red devil mascot proudly adorned one wall of a larger structure Carter assumed was the gym.

She parked and went to the school office. An impeccably

dressed woman in her sixties sat at a desk behind the counter. Her hair was silver-gray and an expensive cut. She was already watching Carter when the agent came through the front door. Her expression was friendly but astute.

"Good afternoon," she said. "May I help you?"

"I'm hoping you can." Carter showed her badge. "Agent Lori Carter, FBI."

The woman's eyebrows went up slightly. "Oh, my. We don't get federal types here often. Mostly just deputies. And they tend to be here to pick up their children."

Carter glanced down at the name plate on the woman's desk. "Shirley, is it?"

She nodded.

"Shirley, there's no problem. I'm doing some background for a case. On someone who attended this school, in fact."

Shirley tilted her head. "You don't say? Who's that?"

"William Sutter," Carter told her.

"Ah." Shirley nodded knowingly. "Now, would you be referring to the father or the son? Both were students here in their own time, you know."

"I'm talking about William Junior," Carter clarified.

Shirley's nodding continued. "I thought as much."

"Do you remember him?"

"Oh, yes. I believe I started working here around the time he was a freshman or sophomore." She stopped nodding and shook her head sadly instead. "Such a tragedy, what happened to that boy. His father, too."

"What exactly *did* happen?" Carter asked. Even though she knew the details, she was curious to hear the public version of events.

"Well," Shirley said, "his father died when he was young, for one thing. Then his mother took up with that Shelton character. Errol, I believe. Terrible drinker, that one. He dragged her right along with him into that devil's trap."

"Alcoholism?"

"They like to call it a disease," Shirley said. "It's not like some virus or cancer wraps itself around a fella's hand and lifts that whisky glass, is it?"

"I suppose not."

"It is a lack of discipline. And a lack of faith." She waved a hand. "That's just me, speaking the Lord's truth. Point is, that boy's mother drank herself to death. It wasn't no secret Errol was hard-handed with both her and young William. Most folks figure it was out of grief and anger he did what he did."

"What did he do?"

Shirley cast her a knowing look. "I imagine you already know that or you wouldn't be here."

"That's fair," said Carter. "Let me ask you this, then: any rumors about where he went afterward?"

Shirley laughed lightly. "Oh, my. Rumors? A multitude of them. Not a one of them weeds had any root to them, if you take my meaning."

Carter wasn't sure if Shirley's easy charm was sincere or a smokescreen. Perhaps it was both. She decided to move on. "You wouldn't happen to have a yearbook from that last year William Sutter was here, would you?"

"Why, of course. Give me a moment."

Shirley rose from her desk. She walked to the back of the office and went through a door into a storage room. Carter heard the sound of a metal drawer sliding open and then closed again. A moment later, Shirley emerged from the room carrying a thin, cream-colored book. When she set it on the counter in front of Carter, the agent saw the same red devil mascot emblazoned on the cover right under the year: 1982.

"May I?" Carter asked.

Shirley made a welcoming gesture. "Be my guest."

Carter opened the yearbook. It took only a few moments

to find the senior photos. She turned to the end and back-tracked to the Ss. When she found the photo of William A. Sutter, Jr., she had to resist the urge to smile.

The man who smiled out at her was a young Sandy Banks.

"Handsome, wasn't he?" Shirley said. "In a solid sort of way, that is."

"He had a girlfriend," said Carter. "Someone named Janet?"

Shirley nodded. "Janet Harding."

Carter flipped backward another page. Her finger slid down the names until she found Janet's. An earnest, pretty face beamed outward. Her blond, shoulder-length hair was feathered in the fashion of the early Eighties.

"Poor girl," Shirley said. "She was devastated when William disappeared. In fact, she didn't stay in town long after that."

Carter glanced up sharply. "No? How long?"

Shirley considered a moment. "Left shortly after graduation, if I recall correctly. In fact, if we're talking about rumors and such, there were plenty going around about her at the time. Most everyone thought when she left that she was going to be with Will."

"Why would they think that?"

"It was a natural conclusion, I suppose," said Shirley. "The two were very sweet on each other."

"Is that what you think happened?"

"No, not at all. I think she wanted to get away and find a new start, that's all."

"But not with Sutter?"

"No, ma'am. That was just people wagging their tongues for a bit."

"Do you know where she is now?"

"Nashville, I believe."

"Is her name still Harding?"

"No, she's married," Shirley said. "Her family name is Griggs now."

Carter handed the yearbook back to the secretary. This time, she did smile. "Thank you, Shirley. You've been incredibly helpful."

"I certainly hope so."

Carter left the building. As soon as she started up her rental car, she dialed a number on her cell phone. On the second ring, Danforth answered.

"I've got her," Carter told him. "I've got Janet."

"Well, our drones paid off," Danforth answered. "We've got *him*."

26

Cousin Mayford listened expressionlessly while Sandy spoke. The old man sipped from a tin cup, watching Sandy with intense eyes but never interrupting.

For his part, Sandy stuck to the broad strokes. He went all the way back to his time in the military. Since Mayford was the one who had saved him, he felt his cousin deserved the full truth. When it came time to tell him about the Four Horsemen, Sandy was matter of fact about what he'd done.

If he'd expected surprise or dismay, he would have been disappointed. The same was true if he'd wanted approval or sympathy. Mayford's flat expression never wavered. He gave no sign of his inner thoughts, other than a nod of approval while Sandy described Hank's ranch and the man's contempt for the government. Sandy imagined the two men would have gotten along well.

When Sandy finished, Mayford motioned toward the similar tin cup next to him. "That's a powerful story, son. I imagine it brought on a powerful thirst."

Sandy lifted the cup and sipped the clear liquid. The bite of alcohol stung his throat all the way down and warmed his stomach.

"I'm sorry about your friend," Mayford said. "The soldier."

"Thanks."

"I know he knew the risks going in, but still. Duty is difficult at times."

"It's a slippery thing," Sandy said. He took another sip of the burning liquid.

"That, too," Mayford agreed. "As for those fellas you took care of up there in Washington… well, I think we both know a thing or two about taking a hand in seeing justice done."

"I suppose you're right."

"'Course I am."

Sandy cleared his throat. "So, what's changed around here since I left?"

"Aw, Christ," Mayford said. "Nothing. And everything, just about. That's the nature of time."

"What about Janet? Does she still live in town?"

"Naw. She left shortly after you did. Went to Nashville, way I heard it."

Sandy nodded thoughtfully. Nashville was a big city, but it was a place to start. "Anything else you can tell me?"

Mayford leaned back, thinking. Then he said, "Well, her mother died not long ago."

"When?"

"Like, four months."

Sandy perked up at that. "Did Janet come back for the funeral?"

"She'd have to, wouldn't she? It's her mother, after all."

Sandy considered. If Janet returned to Big Sandy four

months ago, did that mean she got his letter? He sent it to her mother's address a month before that. There was no guarantee her mother would have kept it, or that Janet would have found it when she came back to settle her mother's estate. Still… there was a chance.

"Did you go to the funeral?" he asked Mayford.

The old man shook his head. "I keep my trips into town as few as possible. Supplies every so often, when I have to. There ain't nobody left who I'd need to pay my respect to."

"Then how'd you know about—"

"I grab the newspaper when I go. Good for starting fires, if not much else. Anyhow, I saw the obituary."

Sandy thought some more. Then he asked, "Is she still Janet Harding?"

"No," Mayford said. "I reckon she's married, or at least was, at some point. Newspaper called her Janet Griggs."

Janet Griggs, Sandy thought.

Nashville.

"What are you thinking on, son?" Mayford asked.

Sandy drained the final sip of his drink. The power of the liquor made him cough, which brought a smile to Mayford's lips. When he finished coughing, he wiped the back of his hand across his mouth and plinked the tin cup down onto the wooden table.

"It's good to see you, Mayford," he croaked.

"I'm glad you made it out."

Sandy grinned. "That remains to be seen," he said, his voice still strained.

Mayford shrugged. "It's been almost thirty years," he said.

"True."

"Then I'd say you made it."

"I suppose you're right." He glanced around the cabin. "Do you need anything?"

Mayford shook his head. "I'm in good shape here," he said.

"Like always."

"All right," said Sandy. "Then let's have another drink. After that, I have to go."

26

Agent Carter trailed behind the tactical team as they made their way through the woods. The team leader, an agent named Patrick Brown, had pointed out the barely distinguishable roadway and they'd followed it to a clearing. Once on the other side of the clearing, Brown's fist went up and the squad halted. He made several hand signals and his men fanned out.

Carter gazed through the trees. She could see the outline of a dilapidated cabin. A thin tendril of smoke rose lazily from a pipe above the metal roof. Next to the cabin, a vehicle cover protected what she guessed was a truck of some kind.

The tactical team took up positions in a semi-circle around the home. To the rear of the cabin was a steadily rising hillside. Atop the hill, Brown had stationed a sniper and a spotter. She knew the sniper and the agents on the furthermost ends of the half-circle formation were responsible for watching the rear of the cabin. The rules of engagement were clear—capture was preferable, but no one was to escape.

Once everyone was in position, Brown leaned around the tree he was using as cover and bellowed, "Sandy Banks! This is the FBI! We have the place surrounded! You have one minute to surrender!" Brown paused a few seconds, then shouted, "Exit the building unarmed, with your hands held high! You have one minute!"

The woods fell silent, except for the sounds of a bird call in the distance. Carter strained her ears but heard no movement from the cabin.

After thirty seconds, Brown shouted again. "Sandy Banks! This is the FBI! We—"

A shot rang out, gouging out a chunk of the tree near Brown's face. The team leader flinched as wood shrapnel sprayed his face. He squatted behind the tree, muttering a curse. Then he signaled for the team to return fire.

Carter wanted to countermand his order, but the protest died on her lips amidst the rattle of gunfire. She clenched her mouth shut. Taking Banks alive had been her goal all along, but she couldn't control his actions. Given the man's history, both ancient and recent, Brown had given him one more chance to surrender than he deserved.

She clutched her pistol in her hand and remained behind the thick tree for cover.

The tactical team used measured, controlled bursts to fire and maneuver forward. A few random shots came from the cabin, including one that struck a team member in the hip. The consistent gunfire from the team kept Banks seemingly pinned down. Meanwhile, the manpower noose slowly tightened on the cabin itself.

Carter stayed in a crouch. She hurried from cover to cover, trailing behind the tactical team. Her gun remained in the ready position but she didn't bother to shoot. The rifles the team members carried were far more effective at range. She kept her ammunition in case she needed it at closer quarters.

When the team was within a stone's throw of the cabin, Brown signaled his grenadier. The man used a launcher to send a canister of pepper spray into the cabin. Despite the fact that there was no wind, she could still smell the sharp bite of the capsicum in her nostrils. She hated the stuff, even though she knew it was preferred over the old-style tear gas.

A moment later, the grenadier launched a second canister.

Through the window, Carter could see the hazy, orange cloud filling the small cabin. She shifted her stance and readied herself. If she were a betting woman, she'd expect one of the agents on the flanks to be calling out that Banks was exiting to the rear, despite the challenges there.

Instead, the front door burst open. A figure lurched forward, firing a rifle in her direction. The bullet clipped a nearby tree and whined past her.

The tactical team returned fire. A staccato rhythm of bursts roared up and, just as quickly, ended. The man staggered backward a step and fell over into the doorway. His head and shoulders were hidden from view.

The woods fell silent again. In front of her, Brown removed a set of field glasses from his equipment and peered through them. When he let out a low curse, Carter asked him, "What is it? Banks?"

"I can't tell."

She adjusted her position behind the tree, and waited.

Brown and his team waited for several minutes. Eventually, when there was no sign of movement, Brown gave the signal. A small, masked element approached the house, carefully picking their way from cover to cover. When they reached the downed suspect, one of the men in the element signaled Brown. Carter didn't recognize the motion. She worked her way up to Brown while the team slipped inside the cabin.

"What was that signal?" she whispered, joining Brown behind a fallen tree.

"Male suspect," Brown said, not taking his eyes from the cabin. "Not our primary."

Carter pressed her lips together in muted anger.

It wasn't Banks.

That meant it was Mayford Sutter.

She could already hear Maw's voice castigating her. They'd killed a seventy year old man. The fact he'd fired on them first wouldn't matter to the SAC. Neither would the fact he was squatting on federal land. The only thing that would matter was if she brought in Sandy Banks, dead or alive.

She remained crouched next to Brown while the team continued its meticulous search. She listened while the team leader spoke into his throat mic in short sentences, first confirming no one had fled from the back of the cabin, then that the cabin itself was clear.

Brown rose and began striding toward the cabin. "Second sweep," he commanded. "Tear it apart."

Carter trailed behind, holstering her pistol. She knew the team needed to be thorough. Perhaps there was a hiding place in the cabin. Her gut told her only the old man who now lay deceased in the doorway had been inside that cabin.

She'd missed her chance.

Carter stopped, thinking.

Or had she? If Banks was gone, she knew there was only one place he'd go.

She reached for her phone.

28

When Sandy made it to Nashville, he parked the stolen Ford Escort at the airport. After walking to the terminal, he took a taxi to the main branch of the library. He considered wandering around downtown until he found a phone booth. He didn't know if he'd find one very easily, though. Payphones had become less and less common as cell phones became as much a part of people's repertoires as wallets.

He'd need a phone eventually, but the first goal was to find an intact telephone directory. The library was the best place to search.

The Nashville Main Library had the classic look of early 20th century architecture, rising up regally from the sidewalk, complete with faux-Greek pillars. The inside was spacious with a high ceiling. A wrought iron railing rimmed the second floor walkway, topped with blond wood. While searching for the reference section, he walked past a doorway to an inner courtyard. A large fountain adorned the center.

It was beautiful and peaceful. Sandy let those emotions flow through him. Neither one had been a part of his experience recently.

In the reference section, he located the telephone directories. He grabbed the most recent one and sat down at a study station. He flipped to the Gs and ran his finger down the column until he found Griggs. The number of entries surprised him. Either Nashville was bigger than he remembered or Griggs was a much more common name than he thought.

Two-thirds of the way down the page, he found it.

Griggs, Trent & Janet.

He stared at the names for a long while. Then he reached for a stub of pencil nearby and scrawled the address and phone number on a square of paper. He stood, slipped the information into his pocket, and returned the directory to the rack.

Outside, he wandered the Nashville streets for a while. Eventually, he stepped into a bar. He ordered a beer and sat in the dim corner thinking. He pulled out the slip of paper and stared down at it. Now he was finally here and had a chance to think, he wondered if he should go through with contacting her at all. Instead, he could slip away. Go live a quiet life somewhere else. Leave her alone.

All of these thoughts had come and gone in the past when he considered this course of action. None of them seemed to outweigh his promise to Janet. Or, if he was being completely honest, his own desire to see her.

To *know.*

The stark listing in the phone book had brought home the fact she had a life. Seeing that in print struck him in a real way the theoretical possibility never had. He always knew she had a life of her own, without him in it. Yet, he'd always held out hope maybe she was in a place in her life that had room for him. It was possible, he'd told himself. Perhaps not the most likely scenario, but still… *possible*. He didn't know.

The telephone listing changed that.

Now, he knew. Janet was married or, at least, she was at some point within the last year. He had no way of knowing if it was still true, or if it was a happy marriage, for that matter. He could no longer believe she was alone and unencumbered.

So, what the hell do I do now?

He brooded on that for most of an hour, nursing his beer. Over that time, one premise after another flitted through his mind. In many of them, he was selfishly disrupting a woman's peaceful life over a promise made by lovestruck teenagers. Going to see her was a bad idea in those instances. No good would come of it.

In some, he was reconnecting with the only woman he'd ever loved.

And still did.

His hope was that thinking through all of these conflicting scenarios would cause one of them to ring true. That it would help him make his decision. He tried to sweep aside his own long yearning and the dangerous journey he'd taken to this point. Instead, he isolated things down to that moment when Janet picked up the phone. He focused on that.

What would her reaction be?

Confusion?

Disbelief?

Anger?

Or would it be joy?

He weighed the consequences. If she didn't want to talk to him, what was the damage? A strange, few days of residual emotional impact, at most? Not the end of the world.

But if she *did* want to talk to him… if she *did* feel the same way he felt…

If he didn't call, he'd never know.

Sandy rubbed his eyes. He knew what a hero would do. A

hero would walk away into the sunset, not risking the chance reaching out to Janet might bring her any pain or disrupt her life. He could see the images like a movie in his head. Even heard the brooding music, rising to a bittersweet swell when the hero made the right choice.

And that is the right thing to do, isn't it?

If you love her, you'll do the right thing.

"I do still love her," Sandy whispered to himself, and he knew it was true.

He loved her too much to do the right thing.

Besides, he was no hero.

Sandy stood and drained the last of his beer. He left a tip for the bartender and headed for the door..

On Old Lebanon Road, he found Shane's Classic Barber Shop.

Business was brisk, but the barbers moved with alacrity. He only had to wait thirty minutes before he was in a chair, draped in an apron. He told the barber, a man with a reddish brown beard and a confident expression, what he wanted.

Out came the clipper. Heavy Tufts of hair fell away from his head to pile up on the floor, leaving him with a neatly trimmed inch on top. While he worked, the barber asked him a few innocuous questions. After Sandy gave one word answers, the barber must have sensed he didn't want to talk and set about doing his work in silence. Once he finished with the haircut, he cleaned up around Sandy's ears and neck. Then he turned his attention to Sandy's beard.

"You've got a good one going here," he said, hesitating. "Nice and thick. You sure you want me to take it off?"

Sandy was sure. The beard and long hair were part of his disguise but his pursuers knew it now, so there was no profit in keeping it. Besides, it was more important to look like someone Janet might recognize.

He closed his eyes and nodded. "Clean shave," he said.

The barber buzzed through the thick beard, leaving only stubble. Then he lathered up Sandy's face. With expert strokes, the barber used a straight razor to shave him more closely than he could ever remember.

After wiping Sandy's face clean and adding some sort of mild aftershave or skin tonic, the barber declared him finished. Sandy opened his eyes and stared at the man in the mirror.

"All good?" the barber asked.

He saw the hardness in his eyes and the lines in his face. Still, it was as close to William Sutter as he was ever going to get.

"All good," Sandy agreed.

The barber whisked off the apron. Sandy paid at the register, and tipped triple the cost of the shave and haircut.

Then he left to find a phone.

She answered on the third ring.

"Hello?"

He knew it was her immediately. Her voice had matured, developed a more confident timbre to it, but it was unmistakably hers. Sandy closed his eyes, envisioning her next to Sugar Creek, smiling, her bare feet in the cool water. Her face was dappled with sunlight and shadow as the noon sun cut through the trees.

"Hello," he said, opening his eyes.

"Who is this?" she asked, but he could tell from her tone she suspected she already knew the answer.

"Did you get my letter?" Sandy asked.

He heard a sharp exhale. "Oh my God. It's you."

They were silent for several seconds. Sandy tried to get a

sense of her in that silence, but couldn't pierce it. He was about to speak when Janet beat him to it.

"I got the letter," she said. "It was with my mother's effects."

"I'm sorry about your mom," Sandy said automatically.

"Thank you." Her response was just as rote. Then she said, "Oh, Will. Why are you calling me?"

"I'm here. In Nashville."

"Oh." She didn't seem surprised. "But why?"

Sandy swallowed thickly. "I made a promise," he said. Then, because that seemed an incomplete truth, he added, "And I guess I had to know."

She didn't ask what he wanted to know. He thought he might have heard a hitching sound, as if she were crying or trying not to. Another silence ensued, but this one was shorter.

"What now?" she asked.

"Can we meet and talk?" Sandy asked her.

She hesitated, but finally answered. "All right. Where?"

"Wherever you want."

She was quiet, seemingly to think it over. Then she said, "There's a bar on Broadway. At Fourth. It's called Honky Tonk Central."

Sandy smiled. "That's very Nashville."

"There's three levels," Janet told him. "I like the second story. You can still hear the music from below but, this time of day, it's quiet enough to talk. And there'll be lots of people."

Sandy nodded. That was good. People would make her feel safe.

"I'll be there," he said.

"Okay," Janet said. "Give me an hour or so."

"I'll be there," Sandy repeated, but she'd already hung up.

29

He arrived early, slipping in through one of the many open sliding glass doors along the side of the first floor. A big man in a black cowboy hat belted out a Garth Brooks tune, accompanied only by his acoustic guitar. The packed, late-afternoon crowd sang along joyously.

Sandy found the stairs and made his way up to the second floor. There, several musicians were in the process of setting up on stage. From the languid pace of their efforts, Sandy didn't think their set was going to start anytime soon. The upstairs seating was about half full. Sandy chose a high table near the windows. When the waitress came by, he ordered a beer but, when she brought it, he didn't touch it. Instead, he watched the top of the stairs, barely able to contain his anticipation.

And he waited.

When her head came into view, he recognized her immediately. She wore her hair short, styled in what he thought of as a Dorothy Hamill cut. He remembered briefly she had worn her hair that way until high school, when she decided to grow it out.

The cut gave her an elegant appearance, something that did not surprise him in the least.

Janet reached the top of the stairs. She glanced around the room to locate him. The years may have added lines and weight to her face, but it hadn't dimmed her brightness. Sandy felt a twinge, high up in his chest, that ended in a cool, electric zing. He raised a hand and waved to her. He thought he saw a smile flash across her face when she spotted him. Then she walked his way.

Sandy stood up to greet her. As she drew close, he saw she was smiling, though the smile had a shadow over it. Despite that, the lines it caused were pleasant ones, and they accented her round features. When she was near enough to hug, Sandy hesitated. But Janet threw open her arms and so he stepped into her embrace.

They stood standing next to the table for several long seconds. Sandy squeezed her gently. Tears burned at his eyes.

I can't believe I'm standing here, he thought. *With her.*

A moment later, he realized she still smelled the same.

Reluctantly, he broke away. They looked at each other from an arm's length, awkwardly smiling.

"It's really you," Janet said.

Sandy nodded. "It really is."

"You look good," she told him.

"So do you."

She scoffed. "Please. I've gotten fat."

Sandy shook his head. "You look wonderful," he said.

Janet looked away, either embarrassed or uncomfortable.

Sandy cleared his throat. Then he waved at the table. "You

want to sit?"

"Sure."

They climbed onto the high chairs and sat across the small table. Neither of them seemed able to speak. Finally, Janet opened her mouth to break the silence, but that was the moment the waitress chose to arrive.

"Drink?" she asked.

"Oh." Janet glanced at Sandy's beer and nodded. "Whatever he's having."

The waitress hustled off.

Sandy took a deep breath and let it out. He noticed Janet do the same. "It's a lot," he said. "I know."

"It's *a lot* a lot," she agreed.

"Thanks for coming."

She met his gaze. "I guess I had to, didn't I?"

Sandy thought back to those last few moments he had with her, almost three decades ago. Her earnest admonition he come back to her. His own equally earnest promise.

"I'm sorry it wasn't sooner," he said.

"You don't have to apologize."

He knew she was sincere, but he couldn't stop himself from explaining. "I would have come," he said. "At first, I wasn't in any kind of place to see you, then I got caught up in—
"

She held up a hand. "I meant it. Don't apologize. Don't explain." She shook her head. "We were kids. It doesn't matter now."

"It matters to me."

She smiled sadly. "I don't mean it wasn't real. Or that I've never wondered what might have been. But that was a long time ago."

"I know."

She stared directly at him. "I know why you came, Will. And I'd be lying if I said I wasn't touched. I don't know what you expected to happen."

"I wanted to see you," Sandy said.

"I have a life," said Janet. She leaned forward for emphasis. "A *good* life."

"I understand."

"Do you?"

"Yes."

Sandy reached for his beer and took a sip. The waitress arrived and plunked down Janet's. She took a drink as well. Sandy noticed her hands were shaking slightly.

"I'm sorry," he said. "I should not have come."

Janet drank from her glass. "No, you shouldn't have," she agreed.

"I knew better," Sandy said, "but I did it, anyway."

"Why?"

He forced a smile. "You know why."

Janet didn't answer. Her eyes sparkled with tears. "I waited for you," she said, her voice lowering. "I waited for a long time."

"I believe you."

Janet picked up the cocktail napkin and dabbed at her eyes. "I tried to wait forever, but forever was just too long."

"I know."

Janet glanced away while she attended to her tears.

"How about this?" Sandy asked. "Let's drink these beers in front of us. We'll be two old friends, catching up for a bit. You can tell me about your life, or say anything you want. When we're done, I'll go on my way. You'll never see or hear from me again."

Janet finished wiping at her eyes and set the napkin beside her beer. Then she nodded. "All right." She took another breath and let it out. "Yes, that would be best, I think."

Sandy raised his glass. "To old friends."

Janet lifted her own. "And promises kept."

That made him smile easily, though, in the same moment, he could feel his heart breaking. He clinked her glass and they drank.

"Tell me about your life," he said.

Janet did. Sandy soaked in the details as she shared them. She was married to Trent, who owned a furniture store. They had three children—a daughter and two sons. The daughter was named for Trent's grandmother. The first son was Trent, Junior. The third child was named William.

A bittersweet pang struck Sandy when she told him that. Janet met his gaze but neither of them acknowledged her choice to name her son after him.

After who I *was*, he reminded himself.

She went on to tell him about her career in real estate, which fluctuated between full and part time in accordance with the different stages her kids were at. Now, with all of them self-sufficient, she was working full time again.

He smiled and sipped as Janet described each child and those quirks that made them special. With each small detail and every sip of beer, he experienced two distinct, simultaneous emotions. One was unparalleled joy for her. She had built a happy, rich life for herself.

At the same time, his own heartbreak flowed underneath that joy. He knew, in another world, that happy, rich life could have been theirs, together. If he had known—if he had truly *understood*—life with her was the cost of vengeance, would he still have taken his fishing knife to Errol's throat?

Most days, Sandy would have known the answer was yes.

Sitting across from Janet at this bar, he wavered in that conviction.

"I'm happy for you," he told her.

"Thank you."

"I mean it."

"I know you do." She drew in a wavering breath. She hesitated, and seemed to be debating with herself over something. Then she nodded, and said, "Will, I have to tell you something."

"What is it?"

She stared at him for a long moment, indecision clear in her eyes. She opened her mouth to speak, then shut it again.

"It's all right," Sandy said. "You can tell me."

Janet's expression was pained. She cleared her throat and glanced away. When she looked back, she said, "I want you to know that what we felt for each other when we were kids back in Big Sandy? That was real for me, too. So, I'm sorry."

"For what?" he asked.

"I'm sorry you came here. That you thought it might have been the start of something, instead of the end."

"That's not on you," Sandy said. "If I was being realistic, I would have expected this. But I didn't want to risk *not* coming, even if there was only a small chance…" He shrugged. "I'm glad I got to see you, Janet."

"Me, too." She swallowed hard, and her voice wavered. "I'm sorry it turned out this way. No, actually—I'm not. I love my life. It's a good life. But I *am* sorry time has passed us by. Sorry for what… what never was." She hesitated, and added meaningfully, "And that I have to choose between you and my own family."

Sandy digested her words, and, slowly, he understood. He glanced around the restaurant, then turned his attention back to Janet. "You don't need to be sorry for that," he said gently, reassuring her. "It's not a choice at all. Your life sounds wonderful."

"It is wonderful," she said, her eyes glossing with tears again. "It is."

Sandy reached out and touched her hand. It was the first physical contact he'd made since their greeting. His chest ached to see her torn in the slightest. This was one of the worst scenarios he'd envisioned—hurting her.

"It's okay," he said. "Really. It's all right. You're doing the right thing."

She smiled sadly and squeezed his hand. Then she let go, picked up the napkin and wiped at her tears. She groaned and laughed at the same time. "Look at me. I'm a mess." She pushed back from the table and stood. "I'm going to go to the restroom and clean up a bit. Then we'll talk some more, okay? Finish these beers?"

"All right," Sandy said.

She nodded to him. Then she turned and walked away. Sandy watched her go, wondering for a moment if she really would come back. Crazily, he hoped she did. But it didn't matter. He meant what he said—it *was* okay. She'd told him everything he needed to know.

Their love had been real back then.

And she had a happy life now.

It was enough. More than enough, really.

He watched as Janet walked away. She passed the ladies' room and headed toward the stairs. Despite knowing she'd do so, a final, small spark of disappointment flared in his chest when she rounded the railing and headed down the stairs. She kept her eyes down, not looking up at him again. He wasn't surprised at all. Her words still rang in his ears.

I have to choose between you and my own family.

When he'd heard that, he had understood.

So he knew what was coming next.

Janet disappeared entirely from view.

A moment later, several men in blue raid jackets sprinted up the stairs, weapons out. There were loud shouts as several other undercover agents moved through the crowd toward him while patrons scampered out of the way.

At the same time, a woman in a raid jacket emerged from

the ladies' room, her pistol drawn. She pointed it directly at him. He stared at her as she approached with a resolute snarl on her hard face. He had no difficulty at all recognizing her.

"Hands in the air!" was one of the many directives that came his way, so Sandy slowly lifted them. He kept his eyes locked on the woman as she drew close.

"Hello, Agent Carter," he said.

30

Agent Lori Carter slid the cuffs over the wrists of Sandy Banks and clicked them into place. She took her time, soaking in the satisfaction of the moment. She'd been chasing this man—this murderer—for almost six months. Longer, if she counted the time she and her partner worked on the case in Spokane before everything blew up. Not every case ended with her taking the suspect into custody. The fact this one was ending helped balance the ledger.

Banks said nothing during the arrest. He cooperated with her directives and offered no resistance. After the cuffs were on, Carter waited a minute or so to make sure the support agents were able to get Janet Griggs into a car and away from the location. The last thing she wanted was Banks calling out to her on the way to the transport vehicle.

The woman had done well, especially given the rapidity with which events had come together. One moment, she was living her normal life, working at her real estate office, and the next, she was in an empty conference room being briefed by an FBI agent about a man she hadn't seen in nearly thirty years.

Carter hadn't given her much time to adjust. "When he calls," she said, "act surprised."

Janet shook her head in wonder. "If he calls, that won't be hard."

"He'll call," Carter assured her. "When he does, set up a meet with him."

She saw the hesitation creep onto Janet's face when she suggested this course of action.

"He hasn't been in contact already, has he?"

Janet glanced down, then back up to Carter. "No."

"No phone calls?"

Janet shook her head.

"Emails? Letters?"

"No."

She leaned forward. "Don't think you can lie to me, Mrs. Griggs."

"I'm not."

"You are. I know about the letter he sent to you. The one where he said he was coming home."

Janet's jaw dropped. "How did you—"

"It doesn't matter."

"You… you can't read people's mail," she protested.

"It. Does. Not. Matter," Carter repeated forcefully. "What matters is the choice you make in the next few minutes. You can help a man who has murdered multiple people, a man who is a wanted fugitive, or you can help your family."

Janet stared at her. "How is any of this helping my family?"

"I think they'd suffer if you went to prison for aiding and abetting a criminal, don't you?"

Janet's face fell. "You're threatening me," she said. "I don't like that."

"It's not a threat. It's a natural consequence I thought you should be aware of."

"It sounds like a threat."

Carter shrugged.

Janet considered her words. Then she said, "What would I need to do?"

"Just set up a meeting. Show up to the meeting so he doesn't get spooked. Talk for a few minutes, then excuse yourself to use the restroom. Walk out of the place instead."

"That's it?"

Carter nodded. "We'll be going in as you're coming out. Plus, we'll have people inside, undercover. It'll be perfectly safe."

"I'm not worried about Will hurting me."

"You should be. He's hurt plenty of people."

"Maybe so, but I'm not worried." Janet looked down at her hands. "That's all I have to do? Be the bait in your trap?"

"And wear a wire," Carter added.

Janet sagged slightly, but she nodded. "All right," she said, resigned. "I'll do it."

Later, while waiting in the restroom stall, Carter had wondered if Janet would follow through. She'd set the trap and arrived as planned, but the conversation droned on much longer than it needed to. As impatient as Carter was to effect the arrest, she supposed the longer the two of them talked, the more relaxed and less suspicious Banks would be. Several of Janet's comments sounded specifically like a coded warning. None were blatant enough to be actionable, but hearing them caused Carter to draw her weapon and prepare to go.

Standing behind Banks now, Carter decided enough time had passed for the other agents to shuttle Janet Griggs away. She nudged Banks forward. They did the slow perp walk to the stairs, down to the first level, and out to the waiting car. Patrons looked on, murmuring in confused amazement. Tactical team members trailed behind her, waiting for Banks to make the slightest aggressive move. In particular, Agent Brown seethed, his anger palpable to her. She knew he was still upset over the members wounded in the shootout with Mayford Sutter. The fallout from that was still coming, she knew. Perhaps it would only amount to a small blip on the national radar, but she also wondered if it would blow up to become another Ruby Ridge or Waco.

That didn't matter right now, however. Right now, all that mattered was she'd captured her man. She put him into the back of the sedan and climbed in next to him. Both remained silent all the way to the FBI field office. There, she finally allowed another agent to escort Banks into an interrogation room while she found an empty desk to make a phone call.

Danforth answered on the second ring. "Yes."

"I have him. Banks. We captured him at a bar on—"

"I'll be there in fifteen minutes," Danforth said.

"What?! You're here in Nashville?"

"Remember our bargain," he said. "I talk to him before anyone else."

"I haven't forgotten, but…" She shook her head, still surprised. "You're already here in Nashville?" Danforth hadn't joined her on the flight to Memphis. When did he arrive here?

"Fifteen minutes," he repeated, and hung up.

Carter replaced the receiver on the cradle, staring down at it. She couldn't shake the feeling that she'd made a mistake somehow, even though she couldn't pinpoint what it was.

31

Sandy sat at the interview table, staring at a slight discoloration on the wall. The events of the last hours swirled through his mind. He was starting to come to the realization that, in a way, this was the inevitable outcome. He couldn't blame Janet in the slightest for her decision, though. If he was being honest, there was a tiny, dying piece of William Sutter somewhere inside him that still felt the sting. That part was almost gone now. And Sandy Banks? He understood it perfectly. She had a family and a life. The people in that life were far more important than a young love from almost thirty years ago.

Truthfully, a fairy tale ending was never in the cards for him. He wished he lived in a world where fairy tales could come true. Wished, in fact, he could will it to be true, much like he and the other Horsemen willed justice into existence.

He knew he couldn't.

Sandy surrendered to that knowledge and his fate.

The door eased open. Brian Moore shuffled in, looking harried and sheepish at the same time. He glanced to the one-way glass window, then back to Sandy.

"Sandy…" he began, then stopped.

Anger welled up suddenly in Sandy. Janet had chosen her family over him. He understood that completely. It was her only real choice. But Brian? He'd turned on Sandy to save his own skin. He'd been a brother in arms, yet he still stabbed him in the back, violating the sanctity of that bond.

"Sandy…" Brian began again, but this time Sandy cut him off.

"Don't say a word to me," he snarled. "Traitor!"

Brian winced as if he'd been struck. "I had no choice," he wheedled.

"There's always a choice."

He shook his head. "Sandy, they already knew everything. Or close enough to it. My only chance was to—"

"You're a piece of shit."

Brian stared at him, somehow shocked at the accusation. Sandy didn't care. His nerves were alive with electric current. He wanted to spring up in his seat and batter his old partner until agents came to his rescue. The longer Brian made excuses, the more Sandy's resistance to that inclination was stripped away.

"*I'm* a piece of shit?" Brian asked.

"A traitorous piece of shit," Sandy clarified.

"What about you?" Brian snapped back. "Look at everything you've done."

"We were Horsemen. They were targets."

"Sure, fine, but not all of those deaths were the same. That woman you shot. Kelly Merchant. She was innocent, Sandy."

"Be careful," Sandy growled. "I have nothing left to lose here."

"Then jump," said Brian.

Sandy tensed in his chair, considering it. "Merchant," he said. "I was tricked into that."

"Were you tricked into shooting the FBI agent? Or that police captain? What about beating those cops in Minneapolis?"

Sandy gritted his teeth. "I did what I had to do. I sure as hell don't have to answer for it to *you!*" The final word exploded from his throat in a ferocious burst.

Brian's shame seemed to have disappeared when he spoke. "They killed your uncle or cousin or whatever, you know. The old man in the woods."

Sandy fell silent. Sadness brushed across his chest.

"Yeah," Brian said. "So, who's the piece of shit now?"

"Maybe we both are," Sandy muttered, but there wasn't nearly as much force behind his words now.

"Maybe so," Brian allowed. "But I'm the piece of shit who is going to have a few years of life on the outside again before I die. Unlike you." Brian glared at him. "And no matter how much of a piece of shit I am, I'll never come close to how terrible you are."

Sandy didn't answer him. Instead, he turned his gaze back to the point of discoloration on the wall. He kept staring at it while Brian seemed to debate saying something further. Eventually, the man turned away wordlessly and left the room.

Five minutes later, Agent Carter entered the room. She carried no paperwork. No file, not even a notepad and pen. She sat down across from him.

"Let me tell you what is going to happen," she began. "First—"

"Your little rat was just in here," Sandy interrupted.

Carter paused. "Brian?"

He nodded.

Carter frowned slightly. "That wasn't me. He was free-lancing."

"That seems to be his thing," Sandy commented dryly.

"It doesn't matter. Here's what is going to—"

"The other agent," Sandy broke in. "Your partner in Spokane. Did he live?"

Carter hesitated, then nodded slowly. "He made it, yes."

"Good."

"No," she snapped. "It is *not* good. He had to take a disability retirement. He has a permanent limp and is struggling to get off the pain pills. Not to mention the PTSD."

"I meant it was good he lived."

"As opposed to what? Actually living his life?"

Sandy didn't react. "I'm sorry," he said, but his words rang hollow even to his own ears. It wasn't that he didn't have remorse. He just didn't know what he could have done differently.

"Fuck your sorry," Carter bristled.

He lifted his hands slightly to placate her and leaned away. "All right, forget I said anything."

Carter glared at him for a few moments. Then she asked, "Did you ever wonder how we got onto you in the first place?"

"I don't care."

"You spent a decade as a Horseman and now you don't care?"

"What does it matter? I'm sitting here, either way."

"If it was me, I'd be curious."

"I'm not."

She nodded slowly, as if digesting that. Then she said, "Of course, if it was me, I'd be full of guilt over the dozens of people I murdered over that time period."

"Those weren't all mine."

"Some of them were."

"Some were," he admitted.

"How many?"

Sandy did some quick calculations. "Nine, that I can remember."

"Including Troy Collins?"

"You already know the answer to that. It was just me and Brian at that point, and you know he didn't do it."

"So, you killed Troy Collins."

"Yes."

"And Kelly Merchant?"

"Yes," he said. "Though that was set up by her husband, Lee. He tricked me."

"Tricked you into murdering her?"

"That's right."

"What about the others, before Collins?"

"Which ones?"

"The bull rider from the year before."

"The one who raped the woman at the stables, you mean? Almost killed her?" Sandy asked. "Yeah, that was mine. Which you already know, courtesy of Brian. Why are you asking me questions you already know the answers to?"

"Why are you so willing to admit to these killings?"

"Why hold back?" Sandy said darkly. "I'm caught. It's over. And you can only hang me once."

The two were quiet for a second. Then Carter's lips parted to ask another question. The door swung open, interrupting her. Sandy turned to see a well-dressed black man in his late fifties saunter into the room. He cast a smile devoid of warmth directly at Sandy.

"Oh, it's not quite over yet," he said.

32

Agent Lori Carter pulled the door to the interrogation room closed behind her as she left. Then she hurried to the adjoining observation room. When she entered, she was mildly surprised to find Mark Szoke standing there, already watching through the one-way glass window.

"When did you get here?"

"Last night," he said, not looking away.

Carter stood next to him, watching through the glass as Danforth settled into the seat across from Sandy Banks. "Same time as him?" she asked.

Szoke grunted affirmatively.

"Jesus, Mark," Carter said. "Don't bowl me over with information here."

Szoke turned toward her with narrowed eyes. "Fuck off, Lori."

She lifted her hands to calm him. "Hey, easy…"

"Easy, my ass," Szoke snapped. "This is *your* fault."

"What's my fault?"

Szoke didn't seem to hear her. "I was happy on a desk, working analysis on the Mexican cartels, minding my own business. Punching the clock. Then you came along asking for a favor and I got sucked right into this, too."

"Sucked into what, exactly?"

Szoke turned to face the glass again, not answering her.

"Mark?" she asked. "Sucked into what?"

Szoke said nothing.

Puzzled, Carter turned to watch the conversation between Danforth and Banks. Danforth did most of the talking. At first, his words were exactly what she expected. In fact, they were some of the same things she had intended to tell Sandy about what was going to happen to him next.

Then, the direction of the conversation shifted. As realization dawned on her, she turned and gaped at Szoke.

"No fucking way," she breathed, seething with anger. "Did you know about this?"

Szoke didn't respond.

Carter lashed out, hitting him in the upper arm with the heel of her hand. Szoke rocked backward, absorbing the blow. "You bastard," she said. "You did know."

Szoke's gaze remained fixed on the conversation inside the interrogation room.

"This is *not* happening," Carter told him. She whirled away and strode toward the observation room door, ripping it open.

A burly man in tactical gear stood in the doorway, an MP-5 dangling chest high from a shoulder strap. The man gripped the handle, his index finger flush to the side of the weapon just above the trigger guard. His expression was hard and impassive.

"Get out of my way," Carter demanded.

"I can't do that," he replied. His voice was as flat and

deadly as his face.

"I am a federal agent. Move, now!"

The man was unaffected by her order. "I think it's best if you wait in the room, ma'am."

"Get out of my—"

"Wait in the room, ma'am," he said.

Carter stared at him in disbelief as a new layer of realization set in. Finally, she stepped backward and swung the door shut in the man's face. She returned to the observation window, standing as far from Szoke as she could while still able to see the proceedings.

"This is not over," she told him in a low voice.

"No," he agreed. "It's not."

33

"As I'm sure you've already concluded," the man who introduced himself only as Mr. Danforth said, "your world is going to change radically from here on out."

"I figured."

Danforth tapped his fingers lightly on the table. "Multiple murder-for-hire cases in Washington," he said. "Enough to get you the death penalty there, even if some liberal judge stays the execution. While you're sitting around waiting for that, how many officer assault cases are teeing up for you in Minneapolis?"

Sandy shrugged.

"I count at least three," said Danforth. "Not to mention numerous stolen vehicles to accommodate your trip here to the fine state of Tennessee."

"The cars are undamaged. The owners will get them back."

"They're still stolen. And what about Agent McNichol?

Will he get his career back?"

Sandy didn't react. "I've already been through this with Agent Carter. What are you, the repeats-everything guy?"

Danforth's cold smile returned. "No, I am most certainly not the repeats-everything guy. Am I to gather, from your responses, you don't need to be convinced the charges against you equate to several lifetimes of incarceration?"

"Consider me convinced."

"Very well, I'll move to the crux of my visit. I am here to offer you a choice. A way out, actually."

"Sure, you are. You're my fairy godmother, right?"

Danforth's smile faded. "No. I am far from that. In fact, if you turn down my offer, you will discover your situation is actually much worse than you realize. You see, I know more than you might think. Not just about Sandy Banks. I know all about Keegan Fuller." He watched Sandy while he spoke. "I know about William Sutter, Junior, as well."

"Good for you. It's not exactly a news flash. It's how you caught me."

"Not a news flash?" Danforth cocked his head. "Perhaps you'll find this newsworthy, then. If you decline my offer, you won't go on trial in federal court. Neither will you be turned over to Tennessee authorities or go back to Washington State, for that matter. Instead, you will be put on a dark trial for all your cumulative transgressions—including illegal warfare in Nicaragua, by the way—and, when you are convicted in that court that doesn't officially exist, you will rot in a black hole for the rest of your life in a place that makes Leavenworth military prison look like an all-inclusive resort."

Sandy soaked in his words. Perhaps it was the shock of everything that had happened over the last hour, but they lacked the impact he expected Danforth wanted them to have. At the moment, the deep, dark hole he described actually sounded almost inviting.

"Am I making myself clear, Mr. Banks?"

"No," Sandy said. "I still don't know what your demand is."

"That's the simple part," Danforth said. "You will simply go back to what you were doing before federal agents interrupted you."

"The Horsemen?" he asked, surprised.

Danforth lifted one shoulder slightly and dropped it. "No, not exactly. And certainly never in Spokane again." He thought for a second. "Or Minneapolis, for that matter. But there are men—and a few women—in this nation who are even more worthy of the particular brand of justice you delivered as a Horseman. We will identify them for you. You will be our sword."

"No," Sandy said.

"Why not? It is surely preferable to the black pit I've described for you, is it not?"

Sandy didn't reply immediately. Then he said, "My life has been full of too much killing and death. Ever since…" He trailed off. "Ever since I was young," he finished.

"It has," agreed Danforth. "As a vocation goes, it quite suits you."

"Go to hell."

"Hell," Danforth said, "is what awaits you if you refuse."

"I'll take the dark hole."

Danforth watched him, almost as if he was gauging Sandy's resolve. The man's sharp intelligence radiated out from his eyes. Finally, he said, "Yours is not the only fate hanging in the balance."

"Who, Brian? Fuck him."

"No, not Brian." Danforth gave him a meaningful stare. "Someone you actually care about."

Sandy shifted in his seat as realization dawned on him. He debated trying to tell the man Janet didn't matter to him, and knew instantly how fruitless a lie that would be. He'd just driven halfway across the country after thirty years, on the off chance things might work out with her.

He remained silent, waiting to see how far Danforth would take things.

"Her cooperation was less than enthusiastic," the man said smoothly. "She could easily be charged with collusion. The charge might not stick, but the damage would be done. I don't know how many people want to buy a house from someone accused of aiding and abetting a murderer."

Sandy didn't answer.

Danforth continued. "Even if she escapes criminal repercussions, getting audited by the IRS year-in and year-out will be its own exquisite pain. These are just the beginnings of what could happen. If I choose, Mr. Banks, I can rain holy hell down on her." He leaned forward. "So, there are really only two questions, aren't there? The first is, do you believe me?"

Sandy stared back at Danforth, taking his turn at gauging how sincere the man was. He saw nothing but cold confidence in the man's eyes. The knowledge he'd displayed, even in this short conversation, told Sandy he had intelligence resources. His threat about the dark trial and the forgotten hole reminded him of how CIA contacts had spoken during his operations in Honduras. Sandy was convinced Danforth was for real. He *could* do what he claimed.

But *would* he?

Underneath the cold confidence in Danforth's eyes, Sandy sensed something else. Call it resolve. Single-mindedness. Or the self-assurance of the zealot. They all added up to the same answer.

"I believe you," he said.

"Good," Danforth replied. "Then we turn to my second question—what's it to be?"

34

Sandy sat rigidly, staring back at Danforth. The man's question hung in the air between them. Sandy could feel the weight of the moment. His decision in the next few seconds would shape the rest of his life.

Not just his, he realized.

Janet's.

That made it no choice at all.

"I accept," Sandy said, the words tasting like ashes in his mouth.

Danforth nodded as if he'd expected nothing less. "Understand what you have just agreed to, Mr. Banks. This leverage I've explained to you remains in place indefinitely. Instead of a life term in prison, you will serve your government, at my discretion."

"I understood the first time."

"Perhaps you did. I prefer to be exceedingly clear early in a relationship to avoid issues later on. So, to be clear: nothing less than your complete and enthusiastic service is acceptable. Any deviation and I will drop the hammer on Ms. Griggs and her family."

Sandy leaned back, suddenly calm again. Now that the path ahead was clear, any remaining anxiety fell away. "There's a saying I heard from a salesman once," he said, giving Danforth a hard stare. "Stop at yes."

Danforth smiled humorlessly. "Indulge me my process, Mr. Banks. I sleep much better at night when I know I have issued a thorough warning."

Sandy waved for him to continue.

"I already mentioned I demand excellent performance from you, not malicious compliance. Beyond that, I should be clear—you don't disappear. Frankly, you don't even *die*. If I believe you half-assed a job and got yourself killed as a form of escape, I will treat that the same as any other transgression on your part. Understood?"

"Yes."

"Good." Danforth hesitated before continuing. "Now, you will be escorted from here to a secure location and briefed further on resources, procedure, and the mundane details of daily living."

"So I'll be under lock and key still?"

"No. By secure, I mean safe and secret. Our contract is now in full force and given the parameters, I don't think we need to worry about secure locations and handcuffs any longer, do we?"

"No," Sandy said. "The invisible shackles you've put in place are good enough."

"I thought so." Danforth stood to go. When Sandy did the same, Danforth held up his hand, motioning for him to sit. "Wait here. Your handler will be in momentarily."

Sandy sat down and cocked his head. "You won't be my

handler?"

"No," said Danforth. "I'll be the one telling your handler what to do."

With that, Danforth left the room.

THIRTY-FIVE

As soon as the door to the observation room opened, Carter closed space with Danforth jabbing her finger at him while she spoke. "You can't do this!"

Danforth spared a distasteful glance toward her offending finger. "Agent Carter, you're mistaken. I just did."

Carter dropped her finger. "What happened to you being small? Without resources? Clandestine?"

"I… may have overstated that a bit."

"Lied, you mean."

"Semantics," said Danforth. "Besides, don't mistake clandestine for a lack of power, Agent Carter."

The anger in her chest flared even higher. "Stealing a prisoner isn't real power," she snapped. "It's bureaucratic bullshit."

"It's a fait accompli, I'm afraid."

"I don't accept that."

"You may have to work that out in therapy, then, because it is already done."

"I'll go to my boss," she threatened, startled by how weak her own words sounded to her. Using Maw as a cudgel wasn't something she was used to. She'd never needed to do it before, either.

Danforth's expression was cool. "I think you'll find Special Agent-in-Charge Maw less than receptive to your entreaties, Agent Carter."

She stared at him, realization sinking in. The system was behind this move, whether she liked it or not. Carter wasn't going to stop it from within.

"I'll blow the whistle, then." Her voice was low and confident. "I'll go to the *New York Times* or whatever. Tell them the whole story, from the murder of Errol Shelton to that shit show down in Nicaragua to the Four Horsemen. All of it."

Danforth appeared unmoved by her threat. "No, you won't," he said confidently.

"Give me one good reason not to," she snarled. "Because you'll kill me?"

"I'll give you three reasons, Agent Carter, and none of them involve your untimely demise."

"I'm all ears."

"One," said Danforth, lifting a single, narrow finger. "As much as the darker machinations of government rankle your idealistic sensibilities, deep down, you know and accept the reality they are a distasteful necessity. To borrow a familiar metaphor, this is how the sausage gets made."

Carter smirked but said nothing.

"Two." Danforth raised a second finger. "You believe in justice, and the greatest justice is the end result."

"That's your definition, not mine."

"It is the only meaningful definition," insisted Danforth

smoothly. "Distributive justice—the fairness of the punishment exacted for the crime—is the only objective measure of justice."

She peered at him, reluctant to be drawn into an academic debate when her ire was up. "You're just trying to distract me," she said.

"No, I am sincerely answering your question. What else matters but that the punishment fit the crime? Certainly not interactional justice—how one is treated throughout the process. That has no bearing on guilt, innocence, or true justice."

"And yet the Constitution—"

"The Constitution is a two hundred fifty year old scrap of parchment that provides three hundred million people with a pleasant fiction. It doesn't grant justice. It creates an illusory set of rules people like you must adhere to and which people like myself quietly ignore."

"I don't accept that, either."

"Your acceptance is irrelevant. These are the realities of our world. Nowhere is that more clear than when one considers procedural justice—that the process was fair. We both know that is a massive illusion. The system is flawed, broken, and, at times, corrupt. People are convicted of crimes they did not commit. They are given inequitable sentences for the same crimes. And..." he paused, wagging his fingers slightly. "...often very guilty people are acquitted due to exploiting one of those rules I mentioned before. People who still need to experience true justice."

Carter crossed her arms. "You're full of shit. I reject everything you just said. And I'm still going to blow the lid off all of this if you don't return my prisoner to me."

Danforth cast her a glance that was almost sad. He lifted a third finger and turned his hand toward her. "You forgot about three."

"What's three?"

"Three is I do not leave anything to chance. Therefore, as of twenty minutes ago, you've resigned from the FBI."

"What?!" Carter gaped at him in disbelief.

"Don't be distressed," said Danforth. "The good news is your application to the CIA was accepted and approved. Fast-tracked, in fact." He smiled at her. "You work for me now."

36

Sandy sat in stunned silence, still processing everything he'd gone through. He marveled at the incredible powerful nature of luck—both good and bad.

On the good, he was still alive and quasi-free, even after all of the close calls he'd experienced since life went off the rails back in Spokane almost six months ago.

On the bad, he remained trapped even deeper into a violent world he'd long wanted to escape.

True, he'd found Janet, and she was happy and living a good life... but he couldn't be with her. Or ever see her again, for that matter.

He'd taken Danforth's deal to protect her and her continued happy blessed existence.

Hadn't he?

The resignation he'd wallowed in just a few short minutes ago had fallen away to something else now.

Resolve.

And, though he hated to admit it, relief.

He knew he had to pay a price for the life he'd led. Now that he was no longer facing the imprisoned fate Danforth described, he was relieved. Killing bad men was better than rotting in a dark pit.

I never should have come back, he knew. *I should have gone to Canada, or Mexico.*

In either place, he could have lived a life in relative peace, much like Hank was doing. Instead, he was going to live in some kind of hell.

Maybe that was his destiny all along. Maybe he was damned as soon as he swung that first stroke with his fishing knife, slashing into Errol's throat, ending him. He never doubted the man deserved it. He'd beaten Sandy and his mother. Worse yet, he was the reason she drank herself into that early grave. Sending him to his own grave was justice.

Now he wondered if it were possible to deliver justice and still be wrong. Certainly, that single moment cost him any life he might have had with Janet. He was plunged into a karmic downward descent ever since, first as Keegan Fuller, now as Sandy Banks.

Sandy clenched his jaw.

Under any name, I probably deserve it.

He didn't know if that were entirely true. He didn't know how much more of a penance he might have to pay for doing the wrong thing to achieve a right outcome. Hell, anymore, he didn't know if any of those outcomes were the right ones.

Janet, he thought.

His promise to her on the banks of Sugar Creek was the promise of a child. He saw that now. Perhaps he'd seen it all along, but just didn't want to admit it. Didn't want to let go of the pure, true feeling he carried for her all those years. However misguided, though, the promise was real. At least, the core of it was. It shouldn't have been about coming back to her. It should have been about protecting her all along.

That was a promise he knew he could keep.

A newfound energy seeped into his limbs. A sense of purpose. He was to become Death once more. As much as he had resisted the role, as much as he had decried the way it made him feel, he knew a part of him had agreed to Danforth's offer so that he could keep doing it.

This is who I am. Even if I hate it.

The door to the interrogation room opened. A new person, a compact man wearing a suit, walked in. He didn't bother to sit nor did he offer his hand. He simply closed the door behind himself and said, "My name is Mark Szoke. I'll be your handler. My word is your law. Get it?"

Sandy nodded his understanding.

"Good," said Szoke. "Welcome to your new life, Sandy Banks."

Afterword

The Last Horseman was published way back in 2010. I am writing this afterword thirteen years later.

That's an incredibly long time to wait for a sequel.

So, my first order of business is to say thank you for being patient. I always knew there were more Sandy Banks stories to be told, but I certainly took my sweet time in getting to them.

Second order of business is to thank Sandy himself.

Wait, what? Thank a fictional character?

Sounds crazy.

Let me explain.

I'm fortunate to have a fan base for my River City novels. Enough of one, at least, that readers ask when the next installment is coming out. Aside from perhaps the spin off series of mysteries featuring Stefan Kopriva, these are just about the only books that readers make noise about wanting the next one as soon as possible. No one clamored for the next book in my hardboiled Ania series or even the next Bricks & Cam Job, which featured action and dark humor. Some have shown excitement for the next Charlie-316 title, but to be fair, that's a co-authored series, so the reach is greater.

No, for the most part, the only "universe" of mine that I hear "what's next" chatter I hear is about River City.

And Sandy.

Funny thing about Sandy Banks. He's been sort of a

"prove it" guy for me.

What do I mean by *that*?

Well, we've all heard the idea that familiarity breeds contempt, right? The same basic concept that leads us to trust an expert over a local source, even if the only thing we can point to that's different is that one lives more than fifty miles away than the other.

I think it's the same when someone knows an author outside of the writerly realm. When that person is a brother, a cousin, a friend, or a colleague, it is sometimes difficult to think of that person as an artist. In my case, the Venn diagram for this phenomenon has three circles.

The first circle is family. When you grow up around someone, it's a little difficult to view them as anything but family. They're just your brother, for instance. I've encountered this reaction with the much of family (with a few glaring, beautiful exceptions—you know who you are!). Even after publishing more than forty novels, many family members still see my career as "Frankie's little writing thing."

I've decided that's fair. I mean, how much depth of attention do I pay to their passions? Probably about the same as they do mine. So it is easy to have that perspective.

The second circle was the people I played hockey with, especially while I still lived in Spokane. For me, the sport was more than just a recreation. My kids played, I coached some, went to games at the arena, followed my team for every game of the season, and played myself.

I played *a lot*. For multiple teams, as a goalie and a skater. So even though I was a cop, most of those folks knew me as a fellow hockey player.

Once again, from their perspective, it's kind of hard to see anything special there. After all, they'd been privy to my poor skating and missed attempts at a glove save. One team watched me put my goalie pads on the wrong legs and play an entire game that way (we won, but still). So, given that level of familiarity, these books I was writing were probably nothing to be impressed about, right?

I decided that was probably fair, too.

The third group was, of course, my professional colleagues. Other cops. Now, believe it or not, cops can be a judgmental group of individuals. And just like those hockey players who played beside me, these fellow officers had seen me up close and personal for over a decade by the time my first crime fiction stories started to appear. That included all of my foibles, certainly, but also simply the reality that I was a regular guy, just like them. Nothing special.

Sure, I wrote a couple of books. But so what? And how could they be any good? After all, much like family and hockey teammates, they *knew* me.

As I said, familiarity breeds contempt.

Now, I'm not going to sit here and try to convince you that I'm a great writer. Or a topnotch storyteller. Not only would that be arrogant, but the truth of the matter is that it's up to you, the reader, to decide how I rate. But I will say that I *think* I'm at least a skosh better than all those family members, hockey pals, and fellow cops expected me to be.

Why do I think that?

Because many have said so. They are the ones who have read my work and been pleasantly surprised. Of course, that's a bit of a left-handed compliment, isn't it?

"Hey, I thought you'd suck, but you're actually not half bad."

But I'll take it. Left-handed or not, it's still a compliment.

So, why thank Sandy Banks for this? Well, more often than not, it has been Sandy Banks who convinced them of this. *The Last Horseman*, much like the sequel you hold now, is a fast read. It is tense and laced with action. And people seem to have liked it. Not only that, but it convinced more than a few Doubting Thomases that… well, that I wasn't half bad.

For most of the reading world, I'm one of a slew of writers out there. Maybe you like my work, maybe you don't. Maybe it's right in your wheelhouse or perhaps it's just not your jam. But you're probably judging based strictly on the work itself. These other folks I've mentioned had to get past knowing me to even get to where you started. They were judging the book by the fact that they know who wrote it, so hard could it have been? And if that's the case, how good could it be?

I'm grateful that Sandy was able to do the heavy lifting to get them past that point and on to "this is actually pretty good."

Like I said, I'll take it.

As for those of you who never doubted, thank you. Your reward, should you choose to accept it, will be a new Sandy Banks novel, *A Hard Favored Death*, in 2024.

And perhaps more after that.

Frank Zafiro
August 9, 2023
Redmond, Oregon

ABOUT THE AUTHOR

Frank was a police officer from 1993 to 2013, retiring as a captain. After retirement, he taught leadership at police agencies across the US and Canada for four years, before retiring completely in order to write full time. He is the author of over forty crime novels.

In addition to writing, Frank is an avid hockey fan and a tortured guitarist. He lives in Redmond, Oregon, with his wife, who remains simultaneously his biggest fan and critic.

You can keep up with him at http://frankzafiro.com.